DYEING DILEMMAS

TALES from the LANDS OF
✤ Arlington Green ✤

BOOK TWO

Stephen B. Allen

Books in the Popular Series
Tales from the Lands of Arlington Green

BOOK ONE: The Road to Nowhere Leads Everywhere

BOOK TWO: Dylan's Dilemmas

BOOK THREE: Death Comes Calling

BOOK FOUR: To the Victor Goes the Toils

BOOK FIVE: The Treasure of the Crimson Corsairs

BOOK SIX: The Further Adventures of the Earl of Barnstable

BOOK SEVEN: Rascals and Royalty

BOOK EIGHT: A King...The Pawn...and Two Queens

BOOK NINE: Sins of the Fathers

Table of Contents

Preface 5
Introduction 9
Unstable with the Horses 15
Fly Away Bird! 23
Something Sure is Fishy Around Here! 41
Wave Your Money Goodbye 53
Breakthrough 71
School Daze 85
Pony Tales 105
Seasonings for the Holidays 119
Construction Destruction 131
Beautiful Music Can Be a Noteworthy Experience 145
Dylan Enjoys a Fling 157
Festive Departure? 181
City Snickers 195

Preface

Fear is a funny thing!

I do not mean to infer that fears are laughable by any means. Some may be unique and quirky, but all are very real and potentially debilitating.

Whether we like to admit it or not, everybody has them. Depending upon the nature and severity of the dread, they can be masked and they may stay hidden...but very seldomly do they completely go away.

Some phobias may be very easy to discern. Should any of the women in my family walk out of the door in the summertime and have a spider end up on their face, the very obvious initiation of intense pandemonium would ensue!

I believe the process would go something like this—there would be a moment of silence until they realize what it is that is crawling across their cheek. Once the shock wears off, high-pitched shrieks of pure terror loud enough to destroy any pocket of silence which may exist within the entire neighborhood would split the air! What follows next is the traditional "Spider On Your Face" dance...which has been handed down from generation to generation for eons (its original point of origin can no longer be determined). The dance begins with the continuation of the shrieking—it may morph into constant moaning at a later point, but the option to revert back to shrieking is always available—followed by the "Slap at Your Face While

Your Entire Body is Shaking and Your Legs Are Pumping Up and Down a Mile a Minute" segment. It is generally at this point where the shrieking reverts to the mournful moaning, with the cries of "Get it off me!" intermixed for our listening pleasure. If she has any prior experience in these matters, her aim is generally good, and the offending arachnid ends up upon the ground—where it is introduced to the bottom of her shoe until there is a sufficient smear of goo visible indicating its demise! Should she be a novice, it is quite possible that her efforts at swatting could result in no spider visible on the ground...which means that it is still somewhere upon her person...which means that the members of the neighborhood who have responded to the shrieking by giving it their full attention are in for a show as items of clothing are rapidly removed until the offender is eventually found and becomes the proper smear of goo! Body shuddering at this point is optional as the command of "Help me get this @$%$@$#$ webbing off!" is given to whomever happens to be nearby picking up the clothes and busy placing them in strategic locations. Once it has been determined that she is now clear of any and all objects even remotely feeling like a spider web, the "Spider On Your Face" dance concludes with the time-honored tradition of blaming the resident male for the spider being there in the first place!

While this scenario *may* have been presented in a humorous tone and *slightly* over-exaggerated, I do believe that I have captured the scene of a fear shared by many fairly well.

But what about the fears which are not so readily observable? Often it is difficult to understand how anybody could be terrified by something which we consider so mundane as to not even be recognized as worthy of fear at any level. Public speakers make presentation all the time before crowds which may number in the thousands...while others cannot handle the anxiety of getting up in a classroom to read a paper they have prepared. Some folks are terrified by dogs, while those of us who have them as pets probably wouldn't understand just how debilitating that could be. Those with Social Phobia can be uncomfortable around people to such a degree that they never even go outside!

Today we have medicines and trained professionals to assist us in dealing with our issues and hopefully help us overcome those fears. People in centuries past did not have such benefits to count on in their fight to break through barriers either self-imposed or otherwise. What they did have, however, was family...their friends...spouses...their faith...and courage.

Or did you think that all of the phobias and fears which plague each and every one of us to some degree just showed up with the advent of child-proof medicine containers and Dr. Sigmund Freud?

Imagine, if you would, a young man from hundreds of years ago during The Middle Ages who—while far from being a coward—tragically lost his parents at a young age. Due this trauma, he cannot find it within himself to easily open up to others emotionally due to his fear of potentially being hurt by them. While gaining confidence in his abilities to deal with exterior situations, it is the interior walls that he has built around himself which he has difficulty in overcoming. For him, placing his trust in another by giving them the power to invade those defenses and open himself to potential scars is something which he struggles with. His inability to conquer this dilemma has reached the point where he finds it nearly impossible to think when in their presence, becoming so flustered and confused that he often is at a loss for words in which to make simple conversation.

And when this person is a beautiful young lady to whom he is strongly attracted?

What...oh what... is poor Dylan to do?

Introduction

This particular saga from my imagination takes place in the early Middle Ages in a land very much like England at a time before guns, colonies, or enlightenment. Feudalism flourishes, countries are run by the Noble-Born in whichever manner they wish—all in the name of the King. While it is a rare time of peace between traditional enemy nations, war always looms on the horizon as local Lords posture for position and wealth. Knights roam the countryside searching for quests in which to earn their honor and glory, or at least a good fight to enjoy.

Life is simple—either you are rich or you are poor. If you have not been blessed with being born into the elite class of Lords and Ladies, there is a very good chance that you are a peasant toiling in the fields for one of them. As a serf, you have virtually no rights; unless you consider working seven days a week a right. For your toil, you're Baron, Earl, or Duke may decide to protect you and your family in the safety of his Manor or with his Knights when war visits his lands… or he may not. You *may* have the opportunity to keep enough of the fruits of your labor so that your family won't starve. And if you are truly lucky, your children shall decide for themselves whom they shall marry.

If the fates have been kind, then you have been born into this world a free man. If so, you have opportunities that mere serfs can only dream of, such as learning trades, earning decent wages for your efforts, and even choosing where you will live. You are free to seek your fortune wherever and however you wish—providing you can get away with it, of course.

Yet, in a world where almost everything about your life is controlled by others, there are some bastions of enlightened thinking where people are not treated like cattle, and where hard work is rewarded and opportunity given to those who truly appreciate its price.

One such place—is Arlington Green.

If you can picture in your mind rolling hills of lush green grass, forests of tall sturdy trees, and fields aplenty nurtured by myriads of ponds, brooks, and streams...then you would have seen the reality of Arlington Green.

To the west of the lands of the Earl of Thornsbury, and a good day's long ride south from the Capital, lie the lands overseen by the Duke and Duchess of Arlington Green. For generations, the Dukes of Arlington Green have toiled to build a haven where their wealth and power are guaranteed not by the threat of the lash. Rather, it is the promise of reward for hard work and loyalty that have brought prosperity to all who call it home.

The village at Arlington Green is typical for the times, with homes made of wood or brick when you could get it and dirt and thatch when you could not. Children carrying more than a day's worth of dirt upon their clothes toil in the fields along with their parents or roam the streets in search of play during the few moments of the day when chores do not interfere. Parents provide and care for the young on the strength of their backs and depth of the calluses on their hands. The smoke of wood fires hangs over the town, along with the aromas of whatever variety of bread is baking in the ovens. Meats are a luxury very few can afford, vegetables are in season when you have grown them, wines are for the enjoyment of the folks who live in The Manor House, and water is clean and drinkable *if* you live *upstream* from the village.

But ale—now *that* is another story. For while smiles are given from the heart, laughter is a precious commodity which lifts the soul and is saved for special events and festivals.

Should you ever happen to travel there, you could not help but notice that the most distinct feature of note is the stone Manor perched upon the crest of the highest hill—which if truth be known is not *all* that high in actuality. It stands above the main village connected by a winding road of dirt, unless it is the rainy season, during which I hope you like mud.

I suppose that some would call it a *castle* as it is made of stone as all good castles are. Yet if judged by size, I would say it would actually be considered more like a large Manor House, with a high surrounding wall of stone. As such, there are no myriad of servants within or soldiers dutifully patrolling its walls. There is, however, a core of Staff Members that reside within The Manor to carry out the wishes of The Duke and Duchess. In addition, there are several people hired from the village to handle the daily tasks such as a laundress or maid.

As some manner of defense is required should the need arise, there is a large (and quite heavy if you have ever tried to move it) iron- reinforced wooden doorway that allows for the only entrance within the surrounding 12-foot high wall of stone.

Upon entering through the gate, you are greeted by a large courtyard with stables off to the right. Should you wander into those stables, you would probably happen across the young stable master Bryce Willis lovingly tending to his horses. Dark of hair, with strong hand and cleft chin, you would be offered a smile from young Bryce or perhaps the happy swishing of the horse's tails if you should happen to be carrying apples in your hand. Had you gone to the left, you would have found yourself entranced by the gardens tended by The Duchess herself, and just may have spied her two boys—sixteen-year-old Tre and Brandon thirteen, wrestling amongst the roses as all brothers do. Dark of hair, Tre is older and taller than Brandon, so he seldom loses. That fact does not interfere with the determination exhibited by his younger blond-haired brother. Often the victor of these struggles is decided by whose clothes are the dirtiest or the number of bruises on their bodies. Today their battles are being conducted under the semi-watchful eye of the Head House Keeper and their former Nanny. Kaye has faithfully served as nurse as well as protector to the children of several generations of Arlington Green's Dukes as did her mother before her. In truth, she is honored to be considered as more a member of the family than a just a person filling a position on The Staff.

Strangely enough, this designation also appears to be given to the other members of The Staff of The Manor as well, as if the bond they all share is one of an extended family rather than a privileged select few sharing a home with people hired merely to carry out responsibilities. And yet they all know very well who is the boss and where they could end up in certain bounds are overstepped.

Depending on the time of day, you may even have seen the rather large bulk of Chef pulling vegetables and herbs from the garden for that evening's dinner.

But if you wish to go straight ahead and enter the house, you will first be "greeted" by the Knight of The Manor, one Sir Preston Monroe. Being in his late fifties, Sir Preston is a bit old for a Knight and has definitely lost a step or two in his gait, which occasionally causes him to trip over things such as his sword—or barrels—or *anything* around him for that matter. Yet being a Knight, there is always some new young armor-clad oaf offering battle who wants to make a name for himself at your expense. Knights generally do not survive to enjoy a ripe old age. Perhaps there is *more* to Sir Preston than meets the eye?

Entering the main house, you would immediately notice that while it is indeed an Upper-Class home, it is far from opulent and garish. The Duke and The Duchess have the trappings that their station in society demands, and yet they do not indulge in all the fancies and fineries that plague so many of their fellow Nobles. They live well, but the blood of their villagers does not flow in any gold or tapestries adorning their walls. Such is not the manner of The Dukes of Arlington Green.

The present Duke is in his early forties, tall, fit, and dark of hair with trimmed beard which is just beginning to carry a hint of gray. When you first meet him, you cannot help but notice the sharpness of his eye denoting inner wisdom and intelligence. While his manner holds more to that of a King than a Duke, he is content with his station in life and has no designs for nor interest in any Throne.

Duchess Caroline by contrast is shorter in stature and thin, yet she carries herself with a presence that indicates wisdom as deep as her husband's with a hint of wit and the love of laughter. She plays a mean game of chess, both on and *off* the board as well, and while she exhibits a great amount of patience, heaven help the person who should get her *too* angry!

Now had you been looking for the *last* inhabitant of The Manor, you would not be alone, for there is work to be done. One would assume that it would be difficult to hide within the confines of so small a town, but then one has obviously never met the object of so *many* such searches.

In his early twenties, he is a bit of an enigma to everyone he meets. Handsome, yet lacking the inner confidence to be vain, his light brown hair is often found stuffed under his old floppy brown hat. Until recently, he had been a traveling Teller-of-Tales, wandering throughout the countryside sharing stories with all who would listen. Being the clever sort, he is actually very good at his craft—just ask him, for he certainly will tell you so. A young man who has never knowingly backed-down from any challenge to come his way, he utilizes his wits and intelligence to overcome any obstacle put in his path. In truth, he is an impish boy who never grew up and now must deal with that most difficult process. Yes, I am referring to the "Storyteller without Peer" who calls The Manor of Arlington Green home.

I am referring to of course…Dylan.

Yes, Dylan, the young Scribe of whom so many things have been written about—by his *own* hand that is. This is indeed the same Dylan who believes that discipline is a merit to be achieved—just at some later date thank you very much. Yes, the Dylan who tries the patience of all those around him, *especially* that of The Duke and Duchess themselves.

That Dylan.

So why does the Duke keep him around, you may ask?

Simple; it is because…well, actually I have no *idea* why.

Just remember that The Duke is a man of wisdom and a good judge of character. Could it be that he sees more in Dylan than Dylan does himself? Why else would he put up with so much nonsense and tomfoolery?

Perhaps by reading the following chronicles you will discover the answer. As you travel deeper into their world, you will laugh…probably at some point despair…and hopefully fall in love with these folks as much as I have.

But I must warn you in advance, for as Dylan *is* the Official Scribe and Story Teller of The Manor, many of these tales are either told from his perspective or narrated by none other than young Dylan himself. Therefore, you should expect a certain…shall we say…*bias* in their telling.

Welcome to The Lands of Arlington Green

Unstable with the Horses

The aroma wafting from the soiled straw perched upon my shovel was a perfect match for the opinion of what I thought of this latest punishment dealt to me. It mattered not that I had justifiably earned the revolting task of helping to clean out the stables several times over for my most recent indiscretions. For a talent such as mine, a hot summer afternoon should be spent down at my favorite fishing spot thinking up new tales and not in the reek that I now find myself in up to the tops of my boots.

"Brother, from what I heard, you are lucky to be getting off easy with only *this* punishment to serve," offered my best friend Bryce as advice in between his loads of clean straw being strewn over the areas which I had reluctantly just cleared. Being the Master of the Stables, Bryce had the luxury of choosing whether he wished to shovel forkfuls of reeking used straw or clean fresh straw for the horse's bedding. Being a wise young man, he naturally chose the latter.

That and there were more than a few paybacks being delivered this day.

"That's easy for you to say," I countered, ceasing my cleaning efforts to lean on the handle of the shovel. The sting of sweat in my eyes made me wipe the sleeve of my tunic across my brow—which unfortunately brought my nose within close proximity of highly soiled gloves—doing nothing to improve my mood in the least!

It was not that I minded helping out a friend, for such is not my way. What irked me so and had really gotten under my skin was the fact that I had gotten caught in the first place. Taking up the handle of the shovel once again, I was about to take my frustrations out on the mass of offal piled in stall number two when a large rat broke from underneath the pile and ran up my leg! Without thinking, I went to swat the animal off of my trousers with the soiled gloves still on my hands. Before the blow could fall, the rodent jumped off and out into the safety of the barnyard leaving this Teller of Tales cursing a blue-streak as I noticed the brown-colored one left behind on my leg for my efforts.

Being the friend that he was as well as a good man by his nature, Bryce refrained from adding to my exasperation by keeping the laughter that he felt about to explode within to himself. This was not an easy task to accomplish by any means with the events playing out in front of him.

"And just how is that easy for me to say?" Bryce inquired as a means to get my mind back on task and out of the doldrums I was rapidly sinking into.

"Because you are used to this...this *job!*" I explained, as I motioned to the stables and its tethered horses about me. "You *chose* this life, whereas I—I should be outside enjoying the glories of nature or at the very least the inside of my closed eyelids as I wrestle with a well-deserved nap somewhere in the cool shade."

"Which is probably where you *would* be," Bryce offered while trying to be heard over the incessant buzzing of the hundreds of flies that called the stables home "if you hadn't gone and done something stupid to raise The Duchess's ire yet again."

A far-off look came to my face only to be replaced by an impish grin as I recalled just what had been done to earn me this trip to the stables.

Knowing that he would never be able to break my spirit or at the very least convince me why I should at least *consider* growing up, Bryce warned

"You had better be careful Brother, or one of these days you're going to push them too far…and then where will you be?" he asked as if to make me see reason.

Remembering enough of my experiences as a wandering Teller of Tales before coming under the employment of the Duke and Duchess made me stop and honestly contemplate Bryce's advice. Deep down I knew Bryce to be right; and yet there is something about my nature that could not allow me to accept losing any challenge that may come my way. Whether that challenge may originate from The Duchess or any other source mattered not, for it was the game and the knowledge that my wits had triumphed that made all of the difference.

"I know you are right, My Friend, and I appreciate your concern and efforts most deeply," I offered as a half-hearted attempt at admitting my error. "And yet it is so difficult for me to be other than I am." Filling the shovel once again with a mixture of old straw and fresh dung, I was about to fling its contents onto our half-full cart when the sound of a female voice directly behind me caused me to stop virtually in mid-air.

"So Dylan," the voice said with an implied casual arrogance as its source exaggeratedly sniffed the air. "One would almost wonder if the odor coming from these stables was due to these horses, or perhaps it is emanating from you who are sorely in need of a bath."

It was her!

A voice so pure could only belong to one woman; the girl that I was certain I had lost forever and was destined never to see again was here! My questing eyes bore into those of Bryce in need of clarification; his smile indicated that yes, I had indeed heard correctly.

Robyn had come to Arlington Green!

I had promised myself that if my prayers were ever answered and I should look upon this most beautiful woman again, that things were going to be different. Dylan was done making mistakes where this girl was concerned; never again would I give her any reason to go storming off needing to get away from me.

I could not think of anything else but that the girl of my dreams was really standing only a few feet away from me. I had to see her; I had to see that what my ears had heard was real. I forgot all of the days I had missed being with her. I forgot how empty I felt inside as our carriages pulled away from Brighton that day. And I forgot that I was holding a shovel-full of steaming horse poop!

Swinging around as quickly as I could in order to see her once again and hold her in my arms, as I swung, naturally the shovel swung with me. Stopping suddenly as she came into view, naturally the shovel which I had forgotten still clutched in my hands stopped with me.

The contents of said shovel, however, did not!

As if time itself had slowed to a crawl, I watched horrified as the smile upon her beautiful face turned into surprise—then shock—and finally into disgust as with a sickening splat heard all the way down into the deepest recesses of hell, the contents of my shovel turned the red frock she was wearing into a red and *brown* frock!

It was difficult to discern which of the two of us was the most stunned by this catastrophe as neither was capable of movement. I looked at her... Robyn stood there staring down at what was dripping off of her dress, her hands outwardly poised as if they could get away from the disgusting mess. She must have detected my surprise when she slowly raised her head so as to face me, her mouth moving as if to speak, but no words could come forth.

I don't believe that she ever saw my head begin to shake back and forth as if to say 'no' as with a cry of pure disgust she stormed out of the stables in search of a water barrel!

Still unable to move as the shock of what had just occurred was having trouble registering with my mind, I stood with mouth agape looking at what was now an empty space until I felt the shovel being pried from my lifeless fingers.

"Brother, you sure do know how to welcome a Lady!" I could hear Bryce say, as he slowly walked to set the shovel back onto the rack of his tools.

Not knowing whether to laugh or cry or go pack my things, I sat upon a bale of hay trying my hardest to convince myself that what had just occurred was beyond the realm of bizarre and must have been my imagination. It wasn't long before the ponderous bulk of Chef arrived at the stables to inform me that The Duke would like to have a word with me and could be found in The Study.

Pausing only to change my clothing and especially the boots, I cleaned up as best I could. Hurrying to The Study, I found The Duke sitting at a table by the window overlooking the garden while going over some correspondence with The Duchess by his side. In spite of the pleasant day and the birds singing outside, I soon discovered that neither the Duke nor The Duchess were in the most jovial of moods.

After letting me stand in silence for what he deemed to be an appropriate amount of time, he never bothered to look up from the papers on his desk to comment "Well, it appears that I need not seek you out to inform you that Robyn has joined us here for a visit." As if listening to someone else speak, I heard myself babbling gibberish involving "I didn't…it happened when…she was there, and I spun, and…" when The Duchess fortunately ended my spewing of nonsense by raising her hand.

"We understand it was an accident," she announced flatly. "Even *you* couldn't be so incredibly foolish."

I was beginning to relax somewhat, when she asked "Dylan, do you remember what transpired the last time you saw Robyn? Do you recall what it was that you asked of me the day of The Music Festival while standing at The Manor gates?"

My answer of I will never forget a single moment of that day brought a smile to her face.

"Then you will remember that you had asked to borrow some money against your future salary in order to buy Robyn a new dress as hers was ruined?"

I told her that I remember it well.

"Good," she replied, "for that is just what we are about to do. It may have been some time passed, but you are going to get the opportunity you asked for and buy her that new dress. And as I have no doubt that your funds for said purchase are non-existent, when we return from town after finding her new dress, I will inform you of how long you will have to work sans salary until it is paid off."

"Didn't you want to buy her new shoes for The Festival as well?" The Duke piped in, obviously enjoying the charade unfolding before him.

"I don't believe I recall that, Sir," I said, knowing how this was about to play out.

"Don't worry," The Duchess reassured us both as she got up to leave; "I do."

Watching as she left us both behind, The Duke finally turned his attention to me still standing before him. "I must say," he announced; "you certainly do know how to welcome a Lady."

"Yes Sir," I replied dismayed by all that had occurred this day; "I hear that a lot."

Later that evening, in spite of having no appetite to speak of, I went to dinner none-the-less if for no other reason than to see what my next six weeks' salary had just bought. Being first to be seated, I had the pleasure of seeing the smirks upon everyone's faces as they entered. Tempted to just get up and leave, I was in the act of pushing my chair away from the table when I heard the swishing of fabric directly behind me. Instinctively knowing it was Robyn bedecked in her brand-new clothes, I slowly turned to face the inevitable.

I had to admit that I had never spent 30 silver sovereigns' so well in my life. She was absolutely stunning!

Making as if to show everyone her new finery, she swirled and twirled about while smiling broadly. Yet nowhere did I detect any overt attempts at belittling me by her actions. What I *did* detect however, was the fact that this dress was lower cut than any I had seen her in previously.

And was it just my imagination, or did it seem that every time she stopped a twirl it was where she was directly facing me?

I have absolutely no idea what we ate that evening, for as Robyn sat to my immediate left at the table, I had difficulty on paying attention to anything other than a feast of 'Fine Breast of Robyn' which I kept glancing out of the corner of my eye. If she had not brought a shawl with her to cover up with, I just may have gotten into even more trouble than I already was!

After dinner, as we walked back towards our rooms, I stopped Robyn and asked if she would sit with me for a while. Finding an out of the way spot in The Library, I lit a small fire after which I offered her what was an honest apology for what had occurred earlier that day in the stables. "I never meant for any of that to have hit you," I told her. "I was trying to… actually, I don't know what the hell I was trying to do! I just want you to know that I would never purposely cause that to happen," I said—all the while doing my best to not look where I was not supposed (?) to be looking.

Telling me that she knows me well enough to realize it was nothing but a stupid accident—emphasis on the stupid part—she thanked me for the lovely dress and especially for sharing those words.

We talked awhile during which I told her how happy I was to see her again. Saying that she felt as did I, she informed me that she was in Arlington Green due to an invitation from The Duchess. When I asked how long she would be staying, she replied that as she had just arrived, she wouldn't commit to any specific length of time right now.

"It really is very beautiful here," she observed. "Or at least of what I have seen of it so far."

"Yes, it *is* very beautiful," I agreed readily. "Much more so than it was even yesterday," I said, which made her smile.

"I've missed you," she said barely above a whisper. "I know that it makes little sense, for we have been together for mere hours, and yet I could not wait to arrive to see you again," I was told to the hint of a blush appearing upon her cheeks.

I told her that I knew exactly how she felt, almost as if an emptiness inside of me has once again been filled at the sight of her. "If it makes you feel any better, I have been absolutely miserable without you," I offered, somewhat pathetically.

"Yes, it *does* actually," she laughed as her hand reached out for mine.

Fly Away Bird!

"I tell you...she is going to drive me stark-raving mad!"

If I was impressing Bryce in the slightest with my tale of woe, he certainly was not letting on as he continued his rhythm of combing his horse Straw Dog without missing a beat. "I've heard it all *before*, Brother," is all that he said to me.

"Yes, I suppose that you have," I admitted as I continued pacing back and forth across stall number three of the stables, "and I'm sure you will hear it again *very* soon once this day has passed! Mark my words, someday you will realize that I'm right...oh yes, you will see that I'm not exaggerating when I tell you that I have tried thousands of times to get along with her...*thousands!*" I exclaimed as I stopped my pacing for a moment before immediately starting right back up again, this time with arms flying about as if to help emphasize my point.

With a heavy sigh born from renewed exasperation, Bryce ceased his currying and turned to face me...except I was no longer there as I had paced all the way to stall number one before returning moments later to continue where I had left off.

"Damn it Bryce, you *know* me; you know I don't like to complain. But with her I just can't help it." At hearing that remark, his eyebrows almost raised themselves right off of his head.

"Okay, what has she done?" he asked, fully knowing that until he did there was no way he would be allowed to continue with his work.

"What has she *done*?" I asked, my irrationality compounding itself by wondering how he could possibly not know as it was so obvious. "My God man, what *hasn't* she done?" I demanded as I stopped my pacing while awaiting his answer. Not receiving any, the pacing began anew all the while muttering to myself "What has she done? What has she *done*?"

"Yes Dylan; what *has* she done? And before you answer, stop that incessant pacing before you wear a trench between my stalls!" he yelled.

Anyone who knows the man will tell you that Bryce does not yell…period! He is about the most even-tempered person you could ever hope to meet, so when I heard him raise his voice, I knew that I was pushing his patience perhaps a little *tiny* bit too far…maybe.

"Do you really want to know what she did, Bryce; do you *really* want to know?" I asked.

"Yes, I really want to know what she did this time," he assured me with a great big lie.

"This time…what do you mean *this* time?" I demanded while giving him first a look of confusion—followed by a look most foul when I discerned his sarcasm.

"What I mean is what has she done since yesterday afternoon when you burst in here and started acting the same crazy way you are now?" he wondered. "And is it the same thing or something different from only the other day when she did whatever you said that she did then? Sorry if I can't remember specifically, but then again there have gotten to be so many instances in the past several weeks since she arrived that they begin to run together into one big blur," he announced flatly. "So I ask you again—what did she do *this* time?"

"You want to know what she did? Okay fine, I'll tell you what she did *this* time! It was um…she did…er…she had the nerve...uh," was as far as I got until I could go no further.

"Can't remember, can you?" he asked, confident of the answer I was going to give.

Stopping my pacing mid-stride, I searched and searched within my mind until I reluctantly gave him the answer he knew was coming. "I *can't* remember—but it must have been something *really* terrible!" was all I could find to say.

He spoke not a word, but his hanging head shaking back and forth spoke volumes.

And then he *did* speak volumes! Wasn't I the guy who gushed about this beautiful girl and how she was just so sweet and wonderful as we shared standing in a sea of mud the day of her performance? And wasn't I moping around whining about never seeing her again all that night long? And wasn't I going to attempt to search in the dead of night throughout Brighton until I found her? I stopped him right there as I had heard more than enough of those "And wasn't" arguments.

"Dylan, what has changed so dramatically in a scant few weeks?" he asked as he went back to his work now that I had stopped acting like a crazy man. An *idiot* perhaps, but no longer a crazy man.

"Bryce, I swear to you I don't know," I told him as I filled Straw Dog's nosebag with oats. "Ever since she has decided to stay, she has changed… *different* somehow; and things are not the same."

"Did you ever stop to consider that perhaps it is *you* that has changed?" he asked without missing so much as a stray hair in Straw Dog's mane.

That question took me completely by surprise. How could I have changed I wanted to know. Or even better, why would I have?

"Because maybe…just maybe when she was only a girl at The Festival she was *safe*. But as she is here now, you are maybe just a bit afraid and running away from letting yourself go and taking a chance with her?" he wondered, all the while fairly certain of the answer in advance.

"So you think I might be trying to distance myself from her by blowing everything way out of proportion to emotionally protect myself?" I asked. I was amazed that as I began to consider the matter, he may have instinctively figured out my actions. Not totally convinced, I had to know. "If that is the truth—and I'm not saying that it may not *be*—even you would have to agree that at times she appears to be overly difficult herself. How would *my* emotional failure be cause for that?" I wondered as I fought to regain some moral ground on which my arguments could stand.

In response, he brought up an excellent point and one worth pondering. "Did you ever stop to consider that she may be doing the exact same thing as you and for the exact same reasons?"

Actually that thought had never even entered my mind. I was just beginning to figure out what I was doing emotionally, and now I'm supposed to figure *her* out as well? The more I considered his words the more I had to agree with him that perhaps *possibly* he could be right about a tiny detail or two regarding his observations.

"I have overheard the two of you when you are working together in creating new songs for her to perform for The Duke and Duchess's guests and you both are quite civil to each other," he observed as with a loving pat to his favorite mount, he made his way to begin attending to the occupant of stall number four. "Why do you suppose that to be?"

Taking a seat upon some crates stacked nearby, I admitted that his observations were indeed accurate as I helped myself to an apple. "Perhaps it is a result of us being creative and thus comfortable in our most enjoyable and natural environments?" I considered. The more I contemplated his words, the more I realized that he was very possibly right.

Answering that I could be absolutely correct, he then inquired how things go when the work has finished.

"That is the truly frustrating part!" I exclaimed as I jumped back onto my feet and began to pace once again. "Once we get past that place where the conversation revolves around our work, I cannot talk to her."

"You mean that either or both of you become instantaneously antagonistic towards the other and the anger begins to flow once again?" he asked as if confused by the concept.

"No…no…no; I mean that I literally cannot *talk* to her," I explained. "As you and I converse openly with each other and say whatever comes to us—when I am not complaining about a certain *someone,* of course—with her I cannot accomplish such an easy task for I cannot think of what to say! I try to talk but become so nervous at the lack of conversation that nothing comes to mind. I know that she is waiting for me to say something as she is equally quiet herself. Soon the silence becomes deafening as both of us realize that, once again, I have failed to do something which sounds so simple yet for me to accomplish with her is so maddening impossible!"

"Why do you suppose that she does not initiate a conversation?" he wondered as he realized that he had just entered the realm between beginning to understand and being completely lost at the same time.

"I do not know," I told him as I sadly shook my head. "I always assumed that she was waiting for me to initiate the conversation, and when I failed once again her silence indicated her disgust. And I really do wish to speak with her—both casually, as well as about matters of the heart," I announced truthfully. "I know it is childish even for me, but I have gone to some amazingly stupid depths just to show her that I am interested in her," I admitted as if pleading my case before a judge.

The angst in my voice clearly indicated to Bryce the truth in what I was saying. The words which I was speaking, however, clearly indicated my stupidity as well.

"Let me see if I get this straight," he offered, the confusion in his voice beginning to lean in the direction of disbelief. "You say that you cannot easily talk to her, and for such she *must* be disgusted with you? And yet, when she reacts in the exact same manner, you fail to recognize that perhaps she is seized by the same affliction as you?" was his observation.

I asked of him if he were capable of answering what was in the hearts and minds of others.

"I have spoken to her upon numerous occasions," he answered while paying no attention to the sarcasm in my voice. "I have found her to be the most wonderful of women—very intelligent and very caring. Why do you refuse to allow yourself to see that within her, expecting only ridicule and insensitivity?" he asked, before immediately proceeding with "And I've heard about the incredibly dumb things you do to capture her attention! Do you really think that helps put you into a better light with her?" he demanded.

His words caused me to reflect upon a time when it seemed that sweetness rained from the very sky itself. Closing my eyes to better remember the day we met, a soft smile came to my face. "I see it within her, My Friend," I admitted as my tone softened dramatically. "It is during those times when once again I feel the way I did the first day we met."

I told him all this as I watched him perform his magic on a horse aptly named Wanderer.

"As beautiful as the first fragile blossoms of Spring after a long cold Winter is how you described her as I recall," he observed as he went about inspecting the shoes upon the bottom of Wanderer's hooves. "Or was my mind addled by all of the ales we drank that night and instead you were telling me the many ways that you found her to be detestable?"

"You know it to be the former," was my reaction—as well as to throw an apple at his head!

Deftly plucking the apple from mid-air, he gave it to Wanderer to enjoy as he then inquired of me "So what has changed?"

"Had I the answer to that, I would not be sitting here talking to you now," I told him as this time I threw two apples figuring that one may get through to my target. This unfortunately was not to be, as I discovered a very interesting item about the man named Bryce Willis that day. I never knew that he was capable of catching apples out of the air equally well with either hand.

As I did not have such ability, I was able to deflect only one of the spheres coming back in my direction as the other got through my defenses to pop me right on the ear!

Laughing hysterically as he observed my reaction, he none-the-less found it within himself to admonish me to watch my language around his horses! Tempted as I was to go into the garden and bring back a pumpkin for him, I restrained myself as I really did wish to talk to him.

I *would* get him back in the near future, however.

Telling me that he had quite a bit of work to complete before sundown, he offered me a challenge—probably hoping that such would hurry the inevitable ending of our discussion. "I'll tell you what; right here and now you admit to me that you are not glad that she is here," he instructed, while pointing his currycomb at me in dramatic fashion. "Say that you care not for her or about her in the slightest and I will speak to The Duke and Duchess on your behalf and request that she be allowed to find employ elsewhere."

"You cannot be serious!" I said, to which he just shrugged his shoulders and went back to his work. "It certainly would allow for things to quiet down around here," he explained his reasoning.

"Never did I believe that you would be capable of such ill will; I am stunned at even the hint of your suggestion!" I fired back, angry at even the notion of what he was implying. "You would force our benefactors to have to choose between the two of us…with one of us having to go back on the road with winter coming? Have you no consideration for anyone at all?" I demanded while getting up to leave, for as far as I was concerned this conversation was over.

Bryce, however, was not.

"Before you go running off all angry and indignant, tell me how it is that you and your actions are not forcing them to make a choice in order to bring peace and calm back to this Manor? Go on Dylan, answer me that. But first, have the guts to explain to me how repugnant I am for saying the words, when you find no fault within yourself for making those very words a reality!"

I made it as far as the stable door before the wisdom of his words hit me right between the eyes. No matter how I did not want to admit it, he was conclusively right. The picture forming in my mind of her wandering through the cold and the snow in search of food and warmth not to mention viable work made me finally realize just how far I had sunk to have allowed our petty arguments to potentially cause such consequences.

Besides, the picture also forming in my mind of *me* wandering through the cold and the snow carrying my bed upon my back was not very pleasant either!

Walking out to the well, I filled several buckets with water which I proceeded to bring back inside of the stables and fill the horse's troughs as if offering Bryce an apology without having to say the words. If he noticed, he mentioned it not but kept about his business of caring for the horses without acknowledging my presence at all. Clearing my throat as a means of capturing his attention did no good, coughing accomplished nothing, even whistling never caused him to look up in the slightest until finally I was forced to capitulate. Offering the apology—which I had to do *twice* as he suddenly developed difficulty with his ears and could not quite hear me the first time, I acknowledged that he was right in damned well nearly all that he had said to me that day.

"So why do you do it, then?" he wondered. When I could not offer an answer, he repeated the question. "Come on, Dylan; answer the question," he demanded this time; "why do you do your best to turn her away?" I got as far as to say I did not know when he stopped listening. Shaking his head back and forth, he repeated his question once again, his anger at my reluctance to answer his inquest building.

"Bryce, I swear I don't kn…"

"Don't give me that garbage! Why do you do it Dylan?" he demanded once more.

Trying to get him to calm down, I tried placating him by offering "I suppose…" but got no further before his voice boomed across the tiny stall.

"I ain't interested in supposes. You tell me right here and now—why do you do it?" he yelled while coming out from behind of Wanderer as if advancing upon me. Honestly fearful as I had never seen him act in this way, I tried to answer how I really did not know when he threw his comb at me with sufficient force to make me duck down or get hit.

"You want to lie to yourself, fine; you go right ahead," he berated me as he continued to draw closer "but you aren't going to lie to *me* any longer! Tell me why!" he demanded once again as he furthered his advance, his eyes full of menace.

"I don't know!" I cried out.

"Tell me why!" he yelled as he was almost within range of grabbing a hold of me. "Tell me why."

Confusion coupled with honest fear of the crazy way he was acting resulted in my being capable of only stammering "I…I don't…"

"Yes you do…tell me why; dammit, TELL ME WHY!" he screamed as he raised his hands as if to grab me by the shirt.

"BECAUSE I'M AFRAID OF DISAPPOINTING HER!" I cried, the truth finally forced out of me as for the first time I understood the reason myself. "Because I'm afraid of disappointing her," I repeated softly, tears falling upon my boots as my head hung in sorrow. "I have spent countless hours dreaming about how wonderful she is to the point that I have created this unrealistic perception of perfection that I cannot match within myself," I sobbed. "No matter what I say or do, it *has* to be wrong; and so I can do nothing."

Having finally begun to understand myself, or at least to be honest with myself, I continued to sob until I felt the strong arms of Bryce encompass me not as if to menace but rather to offer comfort for a painful truth having been ripped out of my soul.

"Forgive me My Friend," he whispered as he continued to hold on. "I had no choice. I could think of no other way to get you to the truth."

Eventually bringing my emotions under control yet still incapable of speaking, the nodding of my head in obvious agreement to his words caused him loosening his arms from about me. Concern for my state of mind was obvious to read upon his face, as he took several steps backward. Croaking out a request for a drink of water, I did my best to regain my composure by the time he had returned. Handing me the cup, I took it in my still shaking hands. It was as I took a drink that my eyes finally met his; I could read relief upon his face, yet his eyes held a deep concern that he had gone too far and a friendship born during days passed had just died upon the floor of his stables!

In answer to his doubts, I embraced him as hard as I was able. "Thank you My Friend…you have done me a great service," I told him much to his relief. Pounding him on the shoulders as he made to walk back to his work, he inquired if I was okay now.

"Do me a kindness?" I asked as a way of answering his question. "Next time should you feel the need to rip a truth from me…any kind of truth… try copious drinks of ale instead!"

I don't know which of us smiled the wider; him for knowing that I was coming back to my old self or me for knowing the same while finally understanding something which had perplexed me far too long.

"That I shall," he promised "as long as you answer me one more question…and don't roll your eyes at me!"

"I am not certain just how much more honesty I am capable of surviving this day," I told him, "but ask away. If I cannot find an answer, I will at least discover if I can outrun you."

"It is not a difficult question I assure you; I even believe you know what I am about to ask," he declared just before he snuck in the equally difficult question of why was I so assured that I would disappoint her…and in what manner?

Pausing only to give him a look frustrating in nature as well as disgusted that he should have maneuvered me to easily, I asked him if he was serious?

"Open your eyes, Man," I cajoled as I proceeded to state the obvious. "She is undoubtedly the most beautiful woman I could possibly imagine—she is talented beyond the measure of myself even on my *best* day—when I observe her when she is not in my company she is sweetness as is described in the best of the love sonnets ever written; I could go on, but you get my point. How could I possibly impress her enough to invest in me emotionally until I was ready to do the same?" I asked as if there could be only one answer to that question.

"You know; I do believe that I would rather spend an entire afternoon with Sir Preston than ask another question of you," he replied. To have made such a statement indicated the high degree of frustration I must be putting him through. "Dylan, you have so many qualities of worth that I am not going to list them at this time; if you would be but honest with yourself you would know this to be true. The only comment I shall make is this; don't you think that she should be free to determine that for herself?"

"It hurts less if I beat her to it," I replied honestly. "If you listened to how I have just described her, could you deal with a woman of such charms determining that you were not worthy?" I wondered, positive that I was right.

"I can understand your reasoning, I truly can," he agreed...*before* he called me a coward.

And a fool!

"If she is as you describe her with such flowery accolades, then tell me this, you cowardly fool (got both of them in there); how could you possibly let her go without fighting for her?"

My extended silence was eventually broken by my declaration that I would rather spend a full *week* with Sir Preston than have to answer even one more of *his* questions!

"Good, for I am beyond exhausted just dealing with you!" he announced. "Go figure out some things for yourself and we will talk again. Just promise me that it will be at the very least several days from now."

Realizing that I did indeed have quite a lot to think about, I thanked him for his patience as well as his wisdom. I told him that he had given me a lot to consider and that I would head down to my favorite fishing spot to do just that. Reaching into the bin in which he kept his clean straw, I pulled out my favorite fishing pole. Waving goodbye, I walked slowly out of the stables and into the courtyard.

Waiting a few minutes after he had seen me exit The Manor's outer door, Bryce called out as if to the very air "He's gone; you can come out now."

The door to carriage number one opened to reveal the figure of Robyn regaining her feet from where she had been concealing herself upon the floor.

"I take it that you heard most of that?" he asked as she came over to stand just where I had stood previously. Failing to receive an answer, Bryce stopped his efforts to look over to where a head full of soft blond hair was nodding in agreement.

"I heard most if not all—some of which I wish I had not," she finally replied. "Bryce…tell me; how it is that he has such a knack for vexing me so?"

"He has a knack for doing that to a great many people and not just yourself," he replied with a grin, only to get serious once more. "Did you gain any insights into the man?" he asked, hopeful for a response both positive as well as encouraging.

Had he been seeking a quick and simple answer, he should have realized no such response would be forthcoming as women are much more complicated than most men. Fortunately, he had plenty of experience with one of the few men on equal footing with them. Realizing that most of his work would not be accomplished that day after all, he motioned for her to take a seat upon a bale of hay as he did the same.

Sighing heavily, she told him that while indeed she had heard what had transcribed, she was still not certain regarding what she had been trying to decide and for which Bryce had arranged our heated exchange just now.

"Since when is there *any* certainty when it comes to matters of the heart?" Bryce asked while secretly wondering if maybe her and I were not in reality twins who had been separated at birth.

"I hear your words and I know them to be true," she answered with a sense of sadness about her. "When I hear *his* words and I want to believe them…I want to believe them very badly," she admitted. "I just don't know if I *can* as I wonder still if he believes his own words as well."

Hearing her honesty as she spoke, he could sense her inner turmoil as easily as he could mine.

"Robyn…I have known a great many men in my day, most of them for much longer a time than I have Dylan, I admit. And yet, I feel that I know him better than I do most if not all of them. And do you why?" he asked.

Neither waiting for an answer nor expecting one, he continued right away with "Because our frustrating friend is the *only* person I know who does not think about what he says! And before you start laughing, that is not my meaning," he warned. "I am not so gifted of tongue as either of you, so I may not be able to convey my meaning precisely, but I do know what I am talking about."

"I have no difficulty in understanding you," she admitted with a smile.

"Good!" he replied, hoping that their discussion did not take as long nor as much out of him as had ours. "Then know this; Dylan does not speak his words...he *feels* them."

"I am afraid that I may have spoken out of turn," Robyn admitted "as I do not gather your meaning to such a curious statement."

"With many people...if not *most* if the truth be known, you feel the need to qualify their words depending upon what you believe they want from you; for does not that describe people in general? Everybody wants something for themselves and will do or say anything to acquire the object of their desires; I am positive a beautiful woman such as yourself *must* have experienced just such folk in your travels," he observed.

"All *too* often!" she gave credence to his statement with emphatic agreement. "Is it any wonder that I have felt the need to create defenses to protect myself?" she asked as if such a concept should be so easily understood.

"Interesting," Bryce declared as he proceeded to study her for her reactions. "And yet you fail to give Dylan understanding to just such mechanisms manufactured to protect *himself?*"

It was now her turn to be lost in contemplation as Bryce's words hit home.

'They really must be twins' he found himself thinking before feeling the need to resume talking in an attempt to be done in time for dinner.

"And yet whether you wish to agree or not, he does not seek to manipulate or take advantage of anyone. In spite of his feelings of being inadequate when compared to others, he requires those he meets—and especially those he knows and places his trust in—to accept him upon his own merits.

It is then that he begins to open himself up and the true Dylan emerges. He will say what he feels and believes in to everyone—everyone with the exception of you, that is," he said after which he paused to allow her to digest *that* one!

Nervously fidgeting, uncomfortable upon her bale of hay as she weighed the merit of his words, it wasn't until she had decided that Bryce was right that she needed to know why.

"Because he has screwed himself up after all this time to the point that he doesn't feel that he can trust you with his feelings as he is certain that you would neither believe what he says to be true…nor care. In the several weeks since you have made this Manor your home, he feels that you should have seen his merits by now and thus would be willing to converse with him—which you are not capable of for the exact same reasoning," he said, shaking his head both in sadness for them as well as trying his best to believe the incredible nature of his discussions this day. "Thus he is forced to try to think about what he wishes to say in order to not make *any* mistakes in his mind for his feelings for you are true, while his frustration tells him that is exactly what he is doing…and thus creating a problem that appears to be nearly insurmountable between you both."

Opening her mouth as if to rebuke what she had just heard, she immediately ceased as she heard her words spoken earlier by the carriage reverberate within her mind. When she did not respond right away, Bryce immediately knew what to say.

"Robyn, answer a question for me, would you please?" he asked to which she simply nodded her head in agreement. "Do I resemble Dylan to you in any manner?" he inquired after which he fell silent.

Inspecting his features for several moments, she eventually replied that he did not look like Dylan in the slightest. Naturally curiosity got the better of her; it was when she asked Bryce why did he ask that question that she wished she had not.

"Because I just opened Dylan's heart to you, and you responded in the same manner of silence as when he attempts to break through and talk to you!" he told her none too pleasantly. "Is it any surprise that he takes such a reaction the way he does?"

Tears came to her eyes as she heard the wisdom of his words. "You were so right when you explained to him that perhaps my defenses are as equally developed as his," she offered as she dabbed at her eyes with the hem of her frock. "I want to be able to believe in him...I find that the more I learn about him and try to see the true Dylan that I *need* to. Yet he makes such trust to be so difficult that I can't release the inner me any more than he can," she lamented, for she really did care for him deeply. Unfortunately, like Dylan himself, neither one knew how to break the cycle which they had fallen into.

"When you seek it honestly, it is not that difficult to find," Bryce told her not in reproach but rather as if teaching her a very important lesson. "If you are unsure about the man, why not ask The Duke his opinion. I have no doubts that he would be more than glad to talk to you and tell you what he thinks," Bryce suggested.

She spoke not a word, but rather nodded her head as if considering his suggestion.

Taking a chance, Bryce now asked her the question the answer to which he had decided necessitated the scene in the stables that day. "Do you still wish me to harness the carriage in the morn and take you away from Arlington Green?" he asked quietly.

She did not answer right away as if her decision was capable of terrible consequence. It was when he finally shook her head 'no' that he found he could breathe once again.

"No, I don't believe that will be necessary," she announced as she leaned over to kiss his cheek.

"Thank you Bryce; I can see why Dylan states that you are a true friend," she said as she rose to take her leave.

"Give the man a chance," Bryce asked as much as suggested. "I promise you that you will not be sorry that you did."

Nodding agreement, she slowly strolled out of the stables lost deeply in thought.

Giving up on the notion of accomplishing anyway near everything he had planned, Bryce decided that he had earned and most decidedly *needed* a large ale after the events of this day. He had not even gotten so far as finishing hanging up his combs when a disturbance at the courtyard door to the stables caught his ear. Turning to face the sound, he spied the form of Robyn standing within the doorway, her hands pointing to the mud still clinging to her dress! Obvious that it had arrived there in the form of a ball of mud, it was equally obvious as to who must have launched said ball.

While she never said it in so many words, her face certainly was sending him the message that she was demanding an explanation of…WELL?!

Doing his best to work up a convincing grin while her eyes bore into his, Bryce threw up his hands in defeat as he said, "And then again…."

Something Sure is Fishy Around Here!

I can't believe that I did such a stupid thing...again!

I realize just how desperate I am to get Robyn's attention, figuring that maybe this will bring about a way for us to begin to relate to each other. But hitting her with a ball of mud? That does not speak of showing interest—that reeks of just the opposite.

Oh, how she must hate me now!

I truly am at my wits end. Having never shared my recurring dreams with anyone—especially not Robyn—deep within my heart, I know that we were meant to find each other. What other explanation could there possibly be? But if my actions are any indication, then I must be stretching Divine Providence's patience to the breaking point!

As with so many times before, once again I wonder how different things could have been between us if I had not turned my head at just that particular moment and never had seen the Mysterious Stranger the day of The Festival of Music? I would have been there when Robyn came off-stage, and...

Then again, what if I had not happened to be sitting on that tree stump amidst the sea of mud just when she was passing by? If I had not been there, chances are we may never have met...or would we have? Perhaps we were fated to happen upon each other later in that day, or even the next day?

Could that be what has happened? Robyn and I were supposed to meet at a later time, and as a result of this mishap, virtually everything having to do with what was to be our relationship has been thrown out of whack? Now, here's a theory that makes sense! One of us was in the wrong place at the right time—thus we met before we were ready—and as a result we are like a half-baked fish.

Wait a minute—that's it!

Fish.

Why didn't I think of this before? Robyn loves fish…while I love *to* fish! I'll go down to the river and catch her a special dinner. That should show her that I was thinking about her and demonstrate that I can be considerate for a change—I'm sure she would appreciate that.

If she survives the shock, that is.

Sneaking into the stables so as not to be seen, I grab my fishing pole from amongst the clean straw and slink out of The Manor as quickly as I can. Breaking into a run once I am in the clear, I head on down to the water as fast as I can go. Finding my favorite spot, I drop my line and wait.

The heat of the day, coupled with the hypnotic sound of water running along the bank, soon soothes me to the point where I find myself nodding. Securing my pole on the off chance that I may end up napping, I settle in. I am just about to fall asleep when the vision of Robyn standing in the middle of the courtyard with mud dripping off of her frock comes back to haunt me one more time.

Between the vision set in my mind and the fact that the fish were not biting, I quickly became melancholy. Reaching for my pole as I was about to give up, I saw the tip of the pole begin to dip slightly in the direction of the river below. I was just able to get my hands upon the pole and gain a good grip when I felt the fish strike! He must have been a good and proper size as he fought me for quite some time before I was able to wrestle him up onto the riverbank and the guarantee of a future poised upon a platter. He was a beautiful fish—and with the help and expertise of Chef, one that Robyn most certainly would enjoy. Once I was able to free my homemade hook from his mouth, I absentmindedly threw my line back into the river—force of habit, I suppose. I was just securing him onto a short length I rope I carry for just such a purpose, when out of the corner of my eye, I once more saw the tip of the pole beginning to dip!

Attributing this action to the current of the river carrying the hook, I nonchalantly pick up the pole in preparation of heading back to The Manor—when I feel the strike of another good-sized fish on the line. The inspiring vision of Robyn enjoying the bounty that I was bringing back for dinner must have changed my luck completely, as within the next hour I had caught six nice fat fish!

Gathering my bonanza, I left the river and was headed back towards The Manor to give Chef the fish for his expert preparation for all of our dinners—when who should I see striding down the path towards the river but The Duchess and Nanny Kaye! There seemed to be a purpose in the way they were stepping lively—which generally indicates some future trouble for Yours Truly. I was able to dash unseen behind a large rock just in time to overhear The Duchess growl to Kaye "I swear…when I get my hands on him…"

Needless to say, I did not stick around to hear any more and risk the possibility of being caught! Ditching all that I was carrying, I managed to throw myself behind a fortuitous thicket just as they were passing my hiding spot. Quiet as a mouse, I slipped away onto an old secondary path and made it back to The Manor in record time.

The look of shock and surprise upon the face of Bryce as I burst into the stables and began filling nosebags with oats as if I had been helping him all day was a priceless experience which I shall never forget!

Upon hearing the approaching voices of The Duchess and Kaye as they returned from their quest empty-handed, I proceeded to hide behind a convenient bale of hay. This action was of course not missed by Bryce—who proceeded to nod his head several times with a wry knowledgeable smile upon his face.

Apparently, my luck was changing—unfortunately, it was changing from bad to worse as I could detect the sound of the voices getting closer as if they were going to next search for me in the stables. Silently pleading with Bryce to save me just one more time, I pointed to the stalls while frantically making the gesture of shoveling. Nodding in understanding, he held up two fingers—meaning I would owe him *two* assists with cleaning the stables for his intercession. The sour look upon my face must have indicated what I thought of his highway-robbery, yet I nodded agreement just the same.

Smiling broadly for having won, he proceeded to casually walk out of the stables towards the sound of the approaching voices.

"Good afternoon, Ladies," I heard him greet them. "Say—would either of you have seen Dylan in the past several minutes?" he inquired.

'Why would he be asking them that?' I wondered, becoming somewhat worried. I really hoped he was not setting me up for having failed to follow through on the last promise I had given him of helping to clean the stables!

In response to his inquiry, The Duchess replied—none too happily, I might add—that they had been looking for me for the past two hours themselves.

"My apologies, My Lady," Bryce offered. "Had I known that you were seeking him, I could have saved you the trouble—for he has been here in the stables helping me for the better part of the day. He left several minutes ago for a brief break, and should have been back by now. That is why I was wondering if perhaps you had seen him."

I could sense the surprise in the voice of The Duchess when she commented that she was not aware that I was on any punishment duty...yet!

"Oh no, My Lady; you misunderstand me," Bryce continued with his own version of 'embellishing the truth'. "He showed up of his own accord to be of assistance. Surprised me quite thoroughly, I must say."

Having no reason to doubt Bryce at his word, the surprise of hearing his story shocked The Duchess so completely that apparently she forgot just why she had been looking for me in the first place! Offering her thanks to Bryce, I could hear the ladies retreating into the garden while calmly discussing nothing more threatening than the color of the roses.

"You *lied* to The Duchess?" I inquired of Bryce upon his return as if he had just performed an act most reprehensible.

"Dylan—in return for *three* assists in cleaning the stables, as long as the fabrication was not of a serious nature, I would have told them anything!"

"*Three*! But you told me two!" I protested.

"See there?" he replied, his voice filled with false piety. "Once you begin the spreading of falsehoods, it becomes so very easy not to know when to stop!"

"I'll not stand for this…this blatant attempt at common *thievery*!" I blustered—to which he just shrugged. "Suit yourself, Dylan," I was told. "I'll just go out and get the Ladies and bring them back with me."

"Are you threatening me?" I demanded.

"Yep."

"You would do that to…to a friend?" I queried, not believing that I was hearing him correctly.

"Yep."

It was at this point that I was forced to capitulate and agree how three really was a very good number. We shook hands on it, but as I knew how in reality he would only get two, the fingers of the hand behind my back were crossed during the effort.

I suppose it is true that the more time one spends with another, the better one gets to know them. This theory was proven to be correct by Bryce admonishing me—sight unseen—to uncross my fingers.

"Come on…you know that I'll be helping you with *two* of them," I admitted.

"I know that," he agreed. "And *you* know that," he admitted. "But what you *don't* know is…I'd have done it for one."

I was shocked! "Really…you would have done it for *one* assist?"

Rinsing his hands off in the water-trough, he asked if I recalled our recent discussion regarding the telling of falsehoods? When I admitted that I did, he casually remarked "Then I guess you will never know for certain…will you?"

The both of us shared a good long laugh over this exchange.

"Come, My Friend," he suggested. "Shall we leave these horses behind and go share an ale? It is almost dinner time after all."

Dinner time?

Oh…no!!!

The Fish!

I had been in such a hurry to escape detection by The Duchess that I had totally forgotten them behind the rock where I had thrown them! Hoping to be able to salvage my catch, I ran back down the path to the rock as fast as my legs would carry me. The smell wafting through the air as I approached their hiding place let me know that the afternoon sun had probably destroyed them beyond saving!

Now, not only was I not going to have the chance to get back into The Duke and Duchess's good graces by presenting them with this bounty, I could not give the best one to Robyn as a way of telling her that I had been thinking of her and that I was sorry for my stupidity…yet again.

Hoping that maybe Chef could still salvage something from my catch, I found a long branch and tied them to it so that I would not smell quite so badly as I slowly trudged back home.

Reaching The Manor just as the sun was setting, I was about to sneak into the kitchen through the side door when I heard Robyn calling me and asking to come over to where she had a small fire going out by the entrance to the gardens.

Doing my best to keep my catch as far *downwind* as I could, I came over and sat next to her. Expecting to listen to her anger, I was shocked to hear her nervously inquire if the Ladies had found me earlier that afternoon. When I informed her that they had not, she genuinely appeared to be relieved.

"When I came inside with the mud still clinging to my dress, The Duchess just happened to pass me in the hall," she explained. "After I answered her question of what had occurred, she flew off in a rage in search of Nanny Kaye—and ultimately you. I had no intention of getting you into any trouble," she admitted as her hand sought out mine.

The flames of the fire danced in the light evening breeze outlining her face against the darkness. Glancing into her eyes that sparkled in the firelight, I had to focus upon what we had just been talking about.

"And yet you had justification to do just that," I told her honestly. "What I did was foolish beyond all measure."

"Now *that* I will not dispute," she laughed—only to become serious once again. "The Duchess…I don't believe that she understands why it is that you do some of the things you do," she told me.

"And you?" was all that I asked.

Gazing long into my eyes, she finally admitted that while she believed that she did, still she could not be completely certain. "Since the day when we met in Brighton, I have found it so difficult to satisfy my doubts about who you really are. The Duchess is beyond certain that you are a selfish oaf capable of thinking only of yourself—but that is not who *I* see."

Thankful beyond words at her opinion, I asked her just what did she see when she looked at me.

Her answer of "A tree," was not exactly what I had in mind.

"You see a tree?" I asked, perplexed.

"Yes...I see a tree. The branches of a tree move in whichever direction the wind happens to be blowing at the moment," she explained while withdrawing her hand to warm it by the fire. "Such is it with you. One moment you appear to be a man warm and caring...and then the wind changes direction and I had better duck for fear of what it carries to smash against my chest! I do not believe there to be malice in your sometimes bizarre actions," she was quick to add. "And I do not believe the opinions of The Duchess to be correct...but I do know that I am getting so tired of attempting to decipher your actions and judging whether they fit with your words."

"Dylan...I need to *know* that I can trust in you. Unfortunately...for the moment...I cannot!" she said as she slightly shook her head back and forth.

We gazed into each others eyes for some very long moments, then both quickly turned to peer back down into the fire in embarrassed silence.

Trying desperately to slow my racing mind in an effort to find some point of reference so as to be able to make a relevant response which would indicate my feelings and bring her some peace of mind, I suddenly remembered how I was going to give her the biggest fish from my catch and had never told her of my intention. All day long, I had thought of her and how I had wanted to treat her as special by giving her that biggest fish.

Have I told you she looks really REALLY good in her new dress?

So here I am sitting next to her, getting more nervous by the minute because I am being so tongue-tied that I could not figure out what to say! I would occasionally glance over at her...she was doing the same to me. Sometimes our eyes would meet—we would smile broadly at each other—then after a few moments of uneasy silence that *needed* to be filled, we would turn back our attention to the fire once again.

This was utter madness! I *had* to break through my inner shell and tell her how I had been thinking of her and that I wanted to treat her to the fish!

I turned back towards her to see her sweet smile once again as the light wind whipped gently through her hair. The rock I was sitting on felt like it was going to cause a permanent indenture on my butt-cheeks, and I knew it was now or never!

Believing that maybe I had found a way to explain myself and indicate the depth of my interest in her, I rose to go retrieve my catch from earlier today. Gathering up all of the courage I could muster, with heart pounding and stomach tying itself into knots, I dropped the fish at her feet as I finally nervously blurted out "You know… these dead fish make me think of you".

You *have* to agree with me that it wasn't my fault… I was just trying to be nice and let her know that I was thinking about her as best I could, right?

WRONG!

It just so happened to be at that moment that Nanny Kaye and The Duchess—who had been out walking in the garden—chanced to meander up to the fire and heard my remark. From the gasps sounding behind me, you would think I had just told Robyn that I think of her as a dead fish!

That's not what I said…as God is my witness, it wasn't my fault!

WRONG!

Small tears began to well up in Robyn's eyes as she rose up as if to flee. The Duchess and Nanny Kaye put their arms around her, and to the sounds of quiet sobbing, the two women led Robyn away into the house. I felt badly as I had wanted to make her feel good; it just got a little messed up…that's all—I had gotten nervous and I *screwed up*.

It would probably all blow over in a minute or two, I reasoned as I poked among the embers of the fire with my stick.

WRONG!

The Duchess with The Duke in tow came purposefully out of The Manor and I swear her feet never touched the ground as she flew across to tower menacingly above me.

Now I've taken many a good chewing out in my time, but I have *never* heard some of the things that were spewing from The Duchess's mouth directed at me! To tell you the truth, some of the names she called me I didn't even *know*.

What was going on here? There was no way that I could get a word in edgewise to explain myself in spite of the number of edges on the sharp words that the Duchess was using! I did interject "But..." a few times, and that was it. I had about as much chance as an acorn at a squirrel festival! My head was swirling from all of the things she was saying to me...and *at* me... and calling me.

Eventually, The Duchess must have gotten tired or called me everything that she could think of, for mercifully her explosion ended with a final "I'm surprised at you! To think you would say such a thing to that sweet girl. I honestly don't know what she sees in you...I really don't!"

Finally, I was left to the crackling of the fire as, in a huff, The Duchess departed to go comfort a very upset Robyn.

Merciful Heavens...I haven't been yelled that much since I was a small boy and convinced Margaret Tanninger that if you looked far enough down a well you could see the Fairy World!

Maybe I am pretty bad at that.

Still shaking nervously from the verbal beating I had just taken, I looked up from the fire hoping to see that there had been no one else observing my chastisement—for I was totally embarrassed. I truly felt terrible as all I had wanted to do was to say something nice to the girl. N*ever* had I expected my innocent gesture to turn out like this!

A clearing of a throat behind me reminded me that I was not alone; I had forgotten the presence of The Duke. Coming around to stand across the fire from where I had slunk down, he just stood there looking at me—not moving except for his head which was going in a constant back and forth motion. He didn't say a word, just motioned with his finger for me to come over to him.

Now what? Was it *his* turn to blast me into oblivion? If I thought I was nervous before, the expression on his face as I drew near brought about downright panic in Yours-Truly!

His voice was very calm and quiet as he spoke. "Go find Bryce and inform him that I would like to have him ready the horses for the coach first thing in the morning."

"You and Bryce will be going somewhere, Sir?" I asked, hoping that I was not being invited to whatever The Duke was plotting.

"No, you and I—and Bryce can do the driving," was his reply.

Oh goody!

Wave Your Money Goodbye

Early the next morning, I was awakened by a knocking on my door. I was happy to see that it was Bryce standing there—until he informed me that The Duke wanted to see me in the courtyard, and that I had best make it quick!

As soon as I could dress, I hurried outside to where The Duke stood waiting next to the coach while Bryce was finishing with harnessing the horses. With no additional words being exchanged, The Duke motioned for me to join him inside and away we went; the Duke on one side of the carriage and me on the other. This was one of the few times that I was going to be allowed to ride *inside* the carriage and I silently prayed that I wouldn't do anything to get in more trouble like ripping the seating from a sharp button on my trousers or something.

After all, it was looking to be that kind of day.

I attempted to begin a conversation when an upraised hand indicated that The Duke was not in the mood for speaking. A large pile of papers sitting next to him on the seat indicated that he had quite a bit of work to do. Having nothing else to do, I took to staring out the window at the scenery flashing past. To my surprise, I saw that we were heading East towards the waters of The Channel that separated our lands from those of our traditional enemies in blue. Turning to ask our destination, I was informed that we were on our way to one of The Channel ports where we would be meeting with a Ship's Captain to discuss the purchase of his vessel.

I knew that The Duke had spoken several times of wanting to establish a trading enterprise; I just hadn't been aware that he was moving forward with his idea. I did find it surprising that I should have been included in the process and could not help inquiring as to why I had been brought along.

"I figured that I could utilize some of your prior experience," he explained. "As I recall, hadn't you told me that at one time, you were in the Royal Navy?"

Trying to remember just which contrived stories I had told The Duke about my past, I answered that indeed I had been in The Royal Navy... sort of.

Cocking his head to one side as if surprised by my response, he asked, "What do you mean *sort of*?"

I explained that the Admiralty had decided that it would be in the best interests of the Nation if I did my service in the secret *Under the Water Boating Service*.

The Duke was amazed that he had never heard of such a group. "I am privy to much of the Crown's military endeavors," he replied somewhat perplexed, "and yet I have never heard of this particular Service. It must be *very* secret!" he observed.

"Yes Sir," I answered curtly; "*very* secret. It was *so* secret that I never even got near any water" I told him while nodding slightly.

The Duke gave me one of his patented 'I know I'm going to be sorry I asked' looks but plowed in anyway. "So how is it possible that you were in the Navy...a branch of the Service that is known for its activity IN THE WATER...and you were in a secret part *of* that Service called the *Under the WATER Boating Service*...yet you say that you *never* got near any water? Just how is that possible?" he asked quizzically, his dark eyes locked into those of his Storyteller.

'*I have him!*' I figured with breathless anticipation. I knew that I would pay for this later, but for one beautiful minute I had reeled in The Duke just like a fish on a hook! Motioning for him to come closer as if there would be the sharing of secret information *so* sensitive that he would be the only one allowed to hear it revealed, I waited until The Duke was poised directly in front of me. "Sir," I whispered, looking furtively back and forth to add more emphasis to this play. "I can't tell you…it's a secret!"

The Duke knew that he had just been had; I even think that he admired the effort that had been put into the story. From the expression on his face, I *knew* that I would pay for what had just been pulled, but decided it was still well worth any future cost.

Fortunately for me, the promise of future retribution was forgotten—at least for the moment—as he informed me that he had also wanted to speak to me regarding another matter. He then asked me how I had been getting along with Robyn these past several weeks?

Here was my chance. I was actually getting an opportunity to speak to someone who would listen! I began to explain what had been happening since she had arrived, the good with the bad. The Duke just listened quietly, his chin resting on his hand. What amazed me afterwards is that an important man like The Duke was really *listening* to me; that in itself was something special.

Miles flew by as to the best of my ability I explained to him our difficulty in relating to each other in spite of how hard we tried. I studied his face for some indication of what his reaction might be. We were passing over a bumpy part of the road, so the slight moving of his head up and down as I completed my diatribe *could* mean that he understood me…or so I hoped. But as of yet, the only sounds to be heard were the steady clip-clopping of the horse's hooves against the roadway, some birds singing off in the distance, and my heart pounding as if to tear out of my very chest!

That, and the growling of my empty stomach as I still had yet to get something to eat.

He gazed at me for a minute before he calmly began to ask some questions.

"Dylan, what does this girl mean to you?" he wished to know.

"Sir, that is the truly frustrating part of this," I exclaimed, "for I am not certain. When I am not with her, I find that I am not happy and want to see her. And yet, when I do, we inevitably end up in some sort of argument. I know what I want her to mean to me; I just can't seem to make that happen."

He chuckled a bit when he said, "If it is any consolation to you, My Boy, you are far from the first young man put in this position by a woman."

"I know that you are trying to help, and I do thank you Sir, but it really isn't any consolation at all," I answered glumly.

"Don't worry, it never has been," he said as if from first-hand experience. If he noticed the nervous wringing of my hands in my lap, he mentioned it not. Nodding his head once again, he offered, "So you do know that in all of your arguments with her that you were wrong, don't you?"

"Yes Sir, I..."

What?

I was wrong? In *every* one of our arguments, I was wrong—every one?

"How could I have been wrong?" I asked with both voice as well as body language.

"Because you were talking to a woman," was all that he said, his answer ending abruptly.

I was totally confused and lost. My eyes darted from place to place within the coach as I fought to make sense of this debacle. Looking back into his eyes which still revealed nothing, I finally found my tongue once again. "I don't understand Sir; I am truly perplexed! How could I have been wrong just because I was talking to a woman?"

He looked long at me with one of those '*You really don't know?*' looks. I could recognize it as such because I get them all of the time. Finally, he spoke. "My Boy, don't you know that any time that you get into an argument with a woman that you are *always* wrong?"

It took a few minutes for *that one* to sink in. I could be right, but I was always wrong?

He could see that I was dumbfounded, for he continued with a wry smile as he leaned forward to attempt to clear up my confusion. "You will never…*ever*…win an argument with a woman. Now I'm not talking about a question such as is there one apple or two apples on a plate," he went on to explain. "One apple will always be one apple; that is a mathematical given. But if you should stray out of that area of absolute fact and get into a discussion attempting logic…believe me, you don't stand a *chance*!" I was told with an emphatic shaking of his head.

"But Sir," I asked him; "isn't that which is right just so and wrong always wrong?" I wasn't phrasing myself very well as I was greatly confused.

"Not necessarily," was his response. " I see that you appear to be lost, so I will try to explain." Bending further forward as if to deliver a truth so profound it would be capable of changing the course of mankind forever, he told me "There are things that are right—and then there are things that are *correct*. You could be 100 percent correct, but if the person you are arguing with is a woman, you will not be right," he explained further. "The reason for this is simply because women are *always* right, and you will never *ever* convince them otherwise. This is a very important lesson for you to learn, My Boy, so pay close attention. You will never *ever* win an argument with a woman, so do not even try!"

Having passed that reality on in conversing to me as if a father to a son, he sat back once again to give me time to dwell upon his declaration.

I was really trying to understand what he was saying, but all of this was well beyond my realm of experience. "So if I understand you correctly, Sir, you are saying that if I am correct then I am not right—simply because I am dealing with a woman who *is* right based solely on the basis that she is a woman?"

"Exactly!" was his response.

"Even when she is clearly not right?" I asked while once again drifting back into the world of total confusion.

"No, she is not *correct...b*ut she is *always* right."

"But who says so?" I wanted to know.

"They do," he replied as if the answer should be obvious.

"Who is they?"

"Who *are* they?" he corrected me. "Why, women of course. They have decided that they are right, and there is *nothing* that you can do to change their minds."

Oh boy; this now getting really confusing! Unfortunately, any further explanation would have to wait as the forward motion of the coach ended indicating that we had arrived at our destination at one of The Channel ports. Instructing Bryce to make himself comfortable as we should be gone most of the day, The Duke gathered his papers into a leather pouch. Together we made our way down to the docks, my vigilance on high alert by constantly checking the skies for diving seagulls. We stopped at the gangplank of one of the many vessels dotting the bay.

We were met by the Ship's Captain, who welcomed us aboard. The wind was whipping the water into small choppy waves as we proceeded to board the vessel—a two-masted schooner named 'The Good Luck Charley'. With the Captain, a crusty old salt named 'Pepper' barking commands to the crew, lines were cast off straightaway as we slowly pulled away from the dock and made our way out into the relatively calm waters of the bay.

Taking our places along the outer rail, I tried to remember where our conversation had ended.

"So you say Sir that I will never be right when arguing with... say a woman like Robyn, correct?" I asked hopefully.

He nodded in agreement.

"So then I will never win," I stated as if I finally understood the message he had been attempting to convey.

"Wrong," was his immediate answer.

It truly was a beautiful day; the smell of the sea permeated everything it touched with an aroma that could take one's breath away. In spite of The Charley heading due East, I was completely lost!

"You look like you are truly confused," offered The Duke with the hint of a smile. "Good…. always remember that feeling, because that is the *exact* feeling that you will get when you argue with a woman."

"But…why would I want to feel this way?" I asked him.

"You don't," was his simple reply.

"So why do it?" I asked.

"EXACTLY!" he exclaimed throwing up his hands as if we had just experienced some sort of breakthrough.

This had to be a bad dream. Please let me wake up!

"Because I'm right?" I replied sheepishly.

"No, you are *never* right, but you may be correct; that is the key. When you're *correct*, you don't have to be right."

Now I had it; it all made sense to me after all. The Duke had been out in the sun too long and had fried his brain!

"It all comes down to the information that you are trying to convey," he continued while paying no attention to the look of complete dismay on my face. "Whether you get credit for that information or not isn't important. What *is* important, however, is making them think that they thought of it in the first place. This way, *you* are *correct, they* are *right*, and what needed to be can be."

I really do have to get this man a hat!

Unfortunately, as the Captain had chosen this moment to give The Duke a guided tour of The Charley, my understanding would have to wait. I remained at my place on the rail trying to decipher all that I had been told.

No matter had many ways I twisted all that I had heard, I was no closer to figuring out the message that The Duke had been trying to share when we made port. The odor of low tide permeated the air as The Charley tied up to the dock. Informing The Captain that he wished to procure the services of a coach, it did not take long for one to arrive. Giving our driver instructions of where he wished to go, The Duke sat back in his seat, gave me a smile, and indicated that he was ready to continue our discussion.

Telling him that I had thought about what he had told me earlier, I had to admit that I could see his point…somewhat. What I could not determine was if Robyn could even care about what I thought or did anymore.

"You really haven't been around women very much, have you?" he asked when I brought up what I had been thinking. "You really don't know that you are in training?" he asked surprised.

"Training Sir?"

"Yes, training…relationship training."

That one hit me right between the eyes! I thought I knew what could have been with Robyn and I, yet I figured by now that she must have given up on any possible relationship growing as it has taken way too long in developing.

"How does one go through this training?" I asked him, completely out of my realm of experience.

"They are very good at this," he told me in a conspiratorial manner. "They—meaning women together—take the unsuspecting fellow, confuse him to no end, and once he gets to the point that he can't tell up from down, they begin to train him in such subjects as how to treat a lady or the consequences of arguing…things like that."

I had to admit that he may have something here; I certainly had experienced all of the required confusion part these past several weeks.

"So what do I do, Sir?" I asked.

Our ride ended outside of the entrance to a small shop with fancy lettering on the front.

"You do what man has done for countless years," he said, opening the door and getting out of the carriage. "You buy her a present."

WHAT?! Me buy her a present…when I am right…er correct…whatever!?

"But why, Sir?" I asked as I followed him to the door of the shop.

"So that you can ask her for forgiveness, of course," was his only answer.

We entered the shop and looked around at pieces of beautiful handcrafted jewelry. The Duke turned to me and said, "You know; you really are going to work for me without pay for a *very* long time."

The shop owner came over, took one look at the two of us standing there, and then turned to address The Duke only. "Sir, how can I help you?" he asked expectantly.

Now The Duke does enjoy some of the privileges that being Nobility brings, but one thing that he absolutely detests is when a person treats another person without respect! I will admit that by the way that both of us were dressed, the shopkeeper obviously reasoned that The Duke was the man with the money and I was probably just his servant. But that is one thing that I admire most about The Duke and Duchess…they don't *have* servants. They have those of us who work for them, but never—ever—do they consider us as servants.

If he did, would we be here now?

"Thank you, but no," The Duke replied as he turned around and walked out the door.

I hurried out after him, leaving the shopkeeper confused and of course without a sale.

"Do you know why I did that?" he asked me as we slowly walked along the quiet street.

"Because you didn't like anything that you saw there, Sir?" I offered while trying to dodge all manner of objects that one would find on a city street.

"No, not at all" he replied. "We left because the shop keeper immediately sized you up as someone he would not like to know yet alone talk to. How did that make you feel?" he asked while studying my face for my reaction.

"Well Sir, to be honest, it is a situation that I have been in many times in the past, so it was not anything new," I admitted. "But to tell you the truth, I do not like it at all! I *know* that I am someone that has a lot to offer and am worthwhile to speak with."

"Precisely! So now you know how Robyn feels."

How in the name of everything that is good did he tie that situation that we just had with anything to do with Robyn?

"Sir, you know that there is nobody in this world that I respect more that yourself, but I just have to ask...have you been out in the sun too long?"

He chuckled a little at that question. "Look at this from her point of view for just a minute," he suggested while still smiling as we walked slowly along. "In *her* mind, she is someone that is worthy to know, has much to offer, and is most worthwhile to speak to. You must understand that, for do you not feel just the same?"

I think I may just be beginning to understand him...somewhat. As we had stopped at what appeared to be yet another store that sold jewelry, I took a moment to verify if I finally understood him.

"So if I may take just a moment Sir, we are going into this shop so that I can get Robyn a gift to make her feel better and get a chance to see that I was correct when I give it to her and explain how I feel, in spite of some of my actions...even though she knows that she is right."

"Almost perfect!" The Duke replied as we stepped into the shop. "Except you left out the part about the apology."

"I know that she will feel badly, Sir, so I really don't expect an apology," I foolishly offered.

"Not her...*you*."

"So I am going to apologize to *her*...because even though I was at least partially correct, I was wrong...solely on the basis that she is a woman... and they are always right," I announced. A smile came to my face, for I believe that I was finally beginning to understand this whole thing.

"Precisely!" exclaimed The Duke. "Now let's find just the right something for her, shall we?"

"Sir, you do realize of course, that I have no money, and indeed owe you my wages for quite a while for Robyn's new dress even now?" I inquired.

Like he would forget...right?

"You owe me 30 silver coins for the dress," was his answer. That makes 6 weeks that you will be working without pay while you pay off that debt."

And here I was going to add to that total; and because I was innocent at that.

I give up!

(It was just at that precise moment that I unknowingly graduated into the next level of training).

We walked through the shop, looking carefully at all of the beautiful items they had for sale. The Duke was looking at the item; I was looking at the prices! There wasn't anything cheaper than at least 50 pieces of silver. Even at that price, I would be adding another 10 weeks of working without pay to my original debt.

Fifteen weeks with no pay! But I knew that I had no choice and would have to get her a present and take the consequences afterwards (up another training level there).

"What is her favorite color?" The Duke asked while looking through the shop's many treasures.

"I believe that it is red Sir, as she certainly seems to enjoy the sight of my blood!" I answered.

That got a chuckle out of him. "Then what do you think of this?" he asked while holding up a golden broach with the biggest red stone that I had ever seen.

"Um…that is pretty nice Sir," I replied, hating to ask the next question but knowing all the time that I would. "How much would that be?"

"This little trinket would be four thousand," he replied nonchalantly.

Four Thousand! Four *thousand* silver coins! I did a quick figuring and desperately realized that I would pay him off in…fifteen some-odd YEARS!

"Might be a bit *gaudy* Sir," I choked. "Perhaps we should look for something a bit simpler?" I offered hopefully

"Of course," he agreed almost absentmindedly. "What do you think about these pearls? They may not be the color red, but they are rather lovely are they not?"

"That they are Sir. And how much would *they* be?"

"Let's see. The price says twenty-four hundred, but I bet that we could get them for two thousand."

I did not have the courage to tell him that not only was 2,000 pieces of silver out of the neighborhood of what I wanted to pay, it wasn't even in the same country!

I frantically looked around the displays until…there it was. I picked up a thin golden necklace on which was set a small red stone; this may work. I looked at the price. Much to my surprise, it was only one hundred pieces. I figured that one up quickly; almost a year of working for free for everything!

'Take your lumps Dylan' I thought; 'you have no choice'.

Another training level completed.

"I think this one would do very nicely Sir, don't you?"

"Very nice…very nice. Good choice." He turned to the shopkeeper: "Wrap this necklace up for us in a red box preferably, and we will also take that strand of pearls there."

WWHHAATT!!! Why both? Did he like me so much that he would make *certain* that I could *never* afford to leave his employ? Somehow I didn't think so, but something was going on here that I did not understand nor like at all.

"Um…Sir; why the pearls?" I asked hesitantly.

Oh please, oh please…be nice!

"These are for The Duchess," he replied sighing while turning over the equivalent of the silver coins in gold to the jeweler.

"Sir, that is a very nice thing you are doing, getting your wife a present just to make her happy," I said while the shopkeeper wrapped up our purchase.

"Nice *nothing!*" he replied. "This purchase is done in the name of survival!"

We received our parcels and left the shop. The driver of the coach must have been following us as it was right outside waiting for us.

Climbing inside, I waited until we had traveled out of the city and were heading back to the dock, when I just had to ask.

"Sir, I didn't understand your answer in the shop; what did you mean by survival?"

"I guess I need to explain that," he chuckled. "I have been married to The Duchess for a number of years now, and I love her dearly. But remember, she *is* a woman. I got her those pearls because when she sees that you came back with a very pretty present for Robyn, she will admire it and instantly begin thinking that it has been a while since I got her anything like that—in which case she will become…*difficult*. Even if she would get over that, when we have the inevitable argument this evening during our walk in the garden, I can give her the pearls *then* rather than do the inevitable and get them for her in a few days and deal with her being…*difficult*… during that time."

"That is what I mean by survival," he announced with finality.

"What argument Sir?" I asked as we arrived back at The Charley. Settling back at our spots at the rail gave us the opportunity to continue our discussion.

"The one where she will say how badly you've acted, in which case I will try to tell her your side of the story, which will inevitably result in an argument! As she is of course a woman, there is no way that I will win, therefore the pearls."

"Sir, you have been extremely kind to me, and an excellent teacher I may add; please don't get in an argument on my behalf. Just tell her that you agree with her and I am a lowly dog or something," I pleaded.

He smiled when I said that. "I appreciate your concern," he told me, "but there is no choice. As a man—with you being a man also—*naturally* I have to take your side, for that is what she is going to expect. If I do *not*, she will think that I am just agreeing with her so as *not* to get into an argument, which will make her even madder. During our 'discussion', in spite of her being right, she will hear information that will clear your name in her eyes. She will of course not tell *me* that, but in the coming days she will begin to speak better of you to Robyn, and this will eventually all blow over. Therefore…the pearls."

I was in the presence of one brilliant man! I did not even deserve an audience with so brilliant a man as I am not worthy.

But one thing was still bothering me. "If I may ask one more question, Sir?" I inquired. "You are a Duke; your word is the law! Can you not just tell The Duchess that you command her to do whatever you desire?"

"Answer your own question," he said as if testing me.

I thought through everything that he had told and taught me this day. The answer came to me amazingly easy.

"Because she is a woman?" I offered.

"Because she is a woman," he nodded.

I told you that he was a brilliant man!

The wind began to pick up as we made our way out of the calm of the bay and into the open water. Under full sail, The Charley proved to be surprisingly quick as she sliced through the waves, soon leaving the crying gulls far behind.

The Captain came on deck and asked if I wanted to take a turn at the helm. "Steer the ship...me?" I asked, amazed that somebody trusted me with such a major responsibility while directly under the eyes of The Duke himself!

"Avast me hearties, keep this heading true," the Captain ordered.

'*Just what does Avast mean?*' I found myself wondering. Unfortunately, The Duke accompanied the Captain below deck, leaving me all to myself.

Taking the wheel from the Helmsman, I set my hands on the pegs while bracing myself against the pitching deck and piloted the ship back towards the dock in the bay and home.

The cry of the gulls mixed with the sting of salt in my eyes made me feel the best I had in many a day. With the ship's wheel in my hands, I felt alive as I maneuvered the sloop between the waves. To my surprise I found that I was pretty competent at handling the ship and was enjoying myself immensely; thus the return voyage appeared to fly by.

Entering the harbor from which we had embarked, I suddenly realized that I had absolutely *no* idea how to navigate the harbor nor how to stop the ship or even slow it down! Looking around in an effort to find the Captain in order to turn the ship back over to him for docking, I realized that he was nowhere to be found. There must have been something very fascinating happening below deck as neither the Captain nor *any* of the crew could be seen!

My repeated calls for help must have been carried away by the sound of the crashing waves as no one came to my aid. I knew that sails had to come down, yet I could not let go of the wheel for even a moment as the current began to increase and we would have ended up jammed upon some of the rocks I could see stirring the waves into a froth directly in our path. Sweat began pouring down from my forehead, the salt stinging my eyes almost to the point of closing. I may not have been able to see the waves crashing against any rocks nearby, but I could certainly hear them well enough. Steering The Charley as best I could by sound alone, initially I was doing fairly well until my vision cleared to the point where I could finally see.

Very quickly I wished I could not!

Able to instantaneously swing the wheel hard to starboard to avoid an outcropping of rock, I knew I would not be so fortunate with the dock looming directly off the bow! No Captain…no Helmsman…no First Mate…no one to be found with a dock getting closer…much closer… REALLY CLOSER…!

With a sickening surety, I *knew* I would never forget the sound of the bow of the ship slamming into the wooden planks of that dock!

Naturally The Captain and the entire crew *miraculously* appeared once we finally came to a full stop. The crew secured the lines to the dock while Captain Pepper and The Duke stood standing at the bow looking down at the damage and speaking quietly. The Captain was gesturing wildly with The Duke slowly shaking his head first back and forth, then finally up and down.

The Duke waved for me to come forward to where he was standing. As I got closer, I began to see just how much damage there was to both the ship and the dock; an awful lot of barnacles would be going hungry until all that damaged wood was replaced!

I stood next to The Duke, but not a word was offered.

The Duke just stared at the damage while saying nothing.

Was I about to be fired? Perhaps thrown to the sharks…or maybe even fired *and* thrown to the sharks? The waiting to find out my fate was pure agony!

The Duke never lifted his head or turned to face me when he quietly informed me "You really are going to work for me without pay for a *long* time, aren't you?"

Finally gathering the nerve to speak, I managed to ask him with much anticipation "How long would that be Sir…exactly?"

The Duke now turned his head and looked furtively back and forth as if this information was highly secret to be shared amongst only the both of us. He waited until I had brought my ear close enough in order to say, "I can't tell you…it's a secret!"

Breakthrough

Upon returning to The Manor, The Duke did not get right out of the carriage. Rather, he placed his hand upon my shoulder for a few last-minute words of advice.

"I understand that you do not wish to bring any attention to yourself for the role you played in saving those children in Brackensburg," he said "and I cannot speak ill of such a decision due to its magnanimity. But consider this," he noted as he picked up his papers and placed them in his satchel; "by telling Robyn the story and especially why you were unable to be with her when she left the stage that day, if that moment was truly the beginning of your troubles as you state, don't you think sharing that information with her could help you two to rise above your difficulties? After all," he said as we stepped out of the coach "only you can answer what the love of the woman whom you yourself declare is the only one for you is truly worth."

Thanking him for all that he had said and done that day, I spied The Duchess waiting for us at the front door. Asking if she knew where Robyn was to be found, she informed me that Robyn was in the Study and wished to see me when we returned. As if that did not sound ominous enough, the look of concern that The Duke gave her over her announcement was answered with the smallest of nods.

Pausing outside the open door to the Study, I checked my pocket once more before stepping inside. The gleam of a blaze in the hearth revealed

Robyn slumped in her favorite chair while intently staring at the fire. Hearing my footsteps, she turned to investigate the sound. Our eyes met; was it hopeful anticipation I can read on her face for I am certain that she could see the same on mine. Our eyes spoke volumes in the deafening silence; the crackling of the fire the only sound to be heard. As if in a dream, I found my feet moving as if on their own as I slowly entered the room and came to sit down next to her.

Fighting the urge to take up staring at the fire as well, I knew that if I did this would end up as just another opportunity lost. Rather I gazed intently into her eyes—which sparkled in the firelight—while telling her how incredibly beautiful she looked when she wore her new dress again last evening.

"It made me think of the first day I met you," I told her: "a vision of loveliness which I will remember always. That day has been recalled in my mind so often that it is hard to realize it had occurred little more than a month ago," I said, my face registering the hint of a smile which my heart just could not share.

Perhaps she could identify with my inner turmoil, for she reached out to take my hand in hers. "As do I," she whispered softly as if afraid by speaking those words loudly that tears would come to her eyes. "It was a very special day—you were so gallant!" she said as she gave my hand a light squeeze.

As if lost in a sea of pleasant memories, we both fell silent; the flames of the dancing fire outlining her face against the darkness.

"I would ask where we lost what had been found that day, but there is no need. I already know the answer to that," I told her. "Were I there when you came off that stage, who knows where it could have lead us?" I offered, as I saw the tears begin to glisten in her eyes. "Instead of what could have been, when I couldn't explain where I had been you lost any faith or trust in me...and rightfully so," I added. "When I saw that you could not believe in me, I lost the same in you; we have been going round in circles ever since, ever hopeful that each new day would bring about a miracle which would finally break the cycle and allow for us to recapture what had been lost. If it is not too late, I am here to offer up that miracle," I told her as I anxiously awaited her response.

The shaking of her head back and forth was what I had been expecting yet had been hoping against. "Dylan," she answered quietly "I am afraid it *is* too late. I don't see how we could hope to recapture that which has been lost, nor am I so certain that we should even try."

My response took her by surprise as I emphatically announced that not only was I certain that we *should* try, but that I was about to do just that!

I could read confusion coupled with uncertainty upon her face as she contemplated my reply. Not waiting to hear her response, I dove right in.

"First and foremost, I am so very sorry for the many stupid stunts I have pulled these last few weeks," I began—when she told me to stop right there as she had heard it all before.

I agreed that she was right; she *had* heard that familiar tune played before. "I will prove to you that I will not need such dramatics or stupidity to gain your attention in the future," I said, hoping that she was still open to hearing what I had to say.

"And just how am I to expect these words to be the truth?" she wondered; "for are not mere words the talent of a Teller-of-Tales? Why should I even begin to place my heart in your hands—regardless of how much I wish I could?" she now asked as her eyes searched mine for some indication that she truly could place her faith in me.

"Perhaps because I am going to break a very important promise to myself," I told her. "I am now going to divulge the secret of why I could not be there when you completed your performance at the Festival. When I have explained to you where I had gone and why, then maybe you will begin to understand my actions and see how my frustrations have lead me to acts of desperation beyond your comprehension," I offered. "More importantly, you will see how they will not need be repeated in the future. But I must warn you that this is a tale long in the telling and difficult to believe. You can take what I am about to tell you on faith, or if that will not suffice, then inquire of The Duke if what I speak is the truth. Either way, at least you will finally know what I have wanted to say to you since that day...that very *special* day."

"Shall I begin?" I asked, hoping beyond reason that she should at least give me the chance to let her see who the real Dylan was. My spirit was buoyed by the nodding of her head 'yes'.

Before I could begin, a knock on the door revealed the bulk of Chef standing there with several plates of food as well as a bottle of wine. "The Duke said you both would probably not be joining us for dinner and suggested that I bring you something," he told us as he set his armload on the table by where we were seated.

Thanking him profusely, it wasn't until he had left and closed the door behind him that I gave Robyn back her hand so she could eat and I began to describe what had occurred that hellish night in Brackensburg. The flames dancing in the fireplace threw ghostly reflections upon the walls of The Study as if we sat amidst that hellhole with the unquenched fires all around us burning people's houses and lives to the ground! Her eyes grew wide in astonishment as I described what became of the town after dark as well as what the roles of both a piece of rope and one indistinguishable Teller-of-Tales meant to those sixteen children.

"Dylan, I *saw* those children the night they performed for the Earl of Brighton and his guests," I was told. "They were just darling! Now I'm not saying that I believe you not, but being on the road, I have met no less than three Tellers-of-Tales who claim to be that man," she told me "and each of them was very convincing with *their* claims."

"And I am certain that you shall hear more of them in the future," I agreed with her. "But how many of them can name each of the children… or sing the song that they were taught to keep their minds off of what was to be seen in those streets?" I wondered. I saw doubt in her eyes until I began to recite the names of those special angels one by one. With each one mentioned, I could see that doubt begin to erode until I saw astonishment register upon her face. Completing the reciting of their names, when I began to sing their song I heard a gasp escape from where her hand rose to her mouth as if to conceal the shock she was experiencing.

"Oh my God!" she exclaimed as her hand fell to her breast "Dylan…I heard them sing that song as they performed for the Earl. I watched as they introduced themselves to an audience ecstatic with applause; not only did you get each of their names right, but you recited them in perfect sequence as well. There can be no doubt," she announced, reality slowly sinking in with every slow nod of her head; "it *was* you!" Reaching once again for my hand, I could read a new sense of pride in the way she looked at me. "Why did you not tell me?" she asked confused.

I explained my reasons for not wanting to bring attention to myself while taking any away from the true heroes of that night.

"I can see one of those heroes before me in this very room," she said with pride coupled with that most sweet smile of hers as she handed me a glass of wine. Did our hands touch longer than was necessary?

Try and explain to me what 'necessary' is some day.

The smell of the smoke from the fire caused the haunting memory of the burning buildings of Brackensburg to flash within my mind. A shiver ran throughout my body as my hand began to shake; if Robyn had not been still steadying my hand I'm certain I would have splashed the contents from the glass onto the floor.

Bringing up her second hand to wrap around mine, her face expressed concern as she asked me what vexed me so. When I explained my actions, she rose from her chair and wrapped her comforting arms about me. I took great strength from her touch, so much that I was able to continue by telling her about the miracle of Holiday Eve. By the time that I had gotten around to what had happened the day of her performance and why I was not there to share with her, I was completely spent!

Sensing that I required a change in scenery, she suggested that perhaps I would care to get some fresh air out in the garden. Thanking her for her being so considerate, I proclaimed that perhaps such action deserved a reward. As we stood, I asked her to close her eyes for me.

I would have expected reluctance to some degree upon her part due to recent history; yet she placed herself totally in my hands as her eyes closed tight.

I couldn't even catch her peeking; what a difference a day made!

Taking her necklace from my pocket, when I held it up to where she could see what I held in my hand, I playfully asked her which frog she would prefer.

I guess that day hadn't made a *complete* difference as her eyes flew open. I guarantee that she never expected to see me holding a small red box in my hands instead!

Confused as to what was happening, it wasn't until I assured her that nothing was going to jump out at her when she opened it that she took the box from my hand. Her eyes shifted from the box to my eyes then back to the box as she began to slowly open it. If she was attempting to get some idea of what the box contained from my expression; I was purposely giving her nothing to go on as my face remained a blank in spite of the excitement I felt.

I can't blame her for feeling shocked as she removed the top of the box and saw its contents. She could not even speak when I asked if she would like for me to put it on her; a nodding of her head was the best she could do.

Taking her soft golden hair in my hands, I was able to set the necklace without fumbling or taking too long; I *may* have snuck a peek at what there was to peek at, however.

"It is so beautiful!" she exclaimed as she held it where she could see the stone and admire it further. "I do not believe that I rate such a gift; or have you forgotten a recent dress presented to me as well?" she asked unable to take her eyes off of the stone as she moved it back and forth along the necklace.

"Well, I had promised you at the Festival that I would purchase such a garment after all," I reminded her which made her giggle. "Consider this bauble as payment for me having waited so long to make good on that promise."

It is not often that I will pass up a meal prepared by Chef, yet that proved to be the case as I found the thought of walking under the stars with a beaming Robyn beyond pleasant. Hand in hand we made our way outside, occasional glances shared brought broad smiles to us both.

Wandering aimlessly once we had gained the cool evening breeze outside, I made the observation that when I had first entered the Study, the expression I had seen upon her face gave me concern. "I was afraid that perhaps I was too late and you had already made up your mind on leaving us," I admitted.

Imagine my consternation when she verified that had indeed been the case. "I was trying to find a way to tell you just that," she said quietly as we strolled with arms swaying to and fro. "I care for you too much to see you so unhappy," she announced as if measuring every word. "I know how I hurt inside and saw the same in you; until I learned the tale of your brave and courageous actions, and you explained why you were missing when I came off that stage, I saw no way for either of us to get beyond our maddening inability to talk to each other."

"And now?" I asked; she must have been able to discern the hope carried in my voice by just those two little words.

Slowly, our measured stroll brought us to one of the benches which graced the garden in the area of the roses. Picking the rose I could discern to be the fullest by the dimmed evening light, I handed it to her as we proceeded to take a seat.

I received a sweet kiss for my efforts; never has a simple flower been appreciated more.

Not sure by which one of us, though.

"There is so much that I did not understand before this evening," she admitted. While her tone indicated relief over misunderstandings explained, there was something in the way her voice dipped at the end; almost as if her heart remained heavy still. The moonlight revealed her to have lowered her head as if not willing to look upon me.

Rather than inquire what was vexing her so, I relied upon some of the wisdom I had garnered earlier in the day courtesy of The Duke. I would not force her to speak about what appeared to be a subject she was reluctant to broach. I would let her decide to open up to me about what was troubling her if and when she was ready—and perhaps, have her gain some trust in me in the process.

Provided that she did not wait *too* long, as seeing her in distress to this degree was very unsettling.

For what seemed like forever, the two of us spoke not, the rustling of the leaves in the trees the only sound to enter out little world. Every few moments she would raise her head as if to look me in the eye once again. I could see her mouth open as if she were about to speak, then all too soon, it would close once again, her head dipping back down as if staring at the rose she held perched upon her lap.

When she finally did speak, it was barely above a whisper. What had been the pleasant and comforting rustling of the leaves in the wind now became an annoyance, as the noise they were making fought for attention against Robyn's quiet words. Incapable of looking at me when she spoke, the rose twirled within her nervous hands.

"Dylan...I lied to you," she told me while returning her gaze to me now that she had finally broken through her emotional defenses. "That very first day in Brighton...when you asked me a question the answer for which I was already struggling within myself to believe or comprehend? When I could not say what was true—as I was certain you would never believe me, I knew not what else to do—so I lied. I have fought with myself over telling you the truth ever since."

"Robyn—be at peace," I told her as my hand found hers...as well as a few thorns from the rose.

"If our meeting upon the mud-flats of Brighton turns out to be as important in our lives as I hope it to be, I cannot imagine how a false answer to any of the myriad of questions I asked of you that day could—or should—be of such importance as to cause you such consternation."

"Your words speak true—yet it is what is hidden within that is so maddening!" she declared upon the verge of tears. "The question you asked of me was a simple one: Did I recognize you? I told you that I did not, yet no sooner did those words escape my lips than I knew them to be false. I had never seen you before that day—of that I am certain," she explained to the shaking of her hand within mine. "And yet, somehow I immediately came to realize that indeed I knew who you were! Where this knowledge came from, I knew not; nor can I find the answer to this dilemma even to this day," she said to the shaking of her head—causing a tear to fall upon my hand.

"I had never met you—never even *seen* you prior to that day," she affirmed "and yet I *knew* you! Help me Dylan!" she pleaded, "for I must gain an understanding of how this could be. No longer can I continue to dwell upon it—or I shall surely lose my mind!"

Upon hearing her words, as if the lifting of a veil which had been covering my eyes, clarity was given to me on so many issues which had been tormenting me as well.

Gathering her into my arms, as I gently rocked her back and forth, I asked her simply "Robyn— do you believe in dreams?"

☩

"And you have had this very same dream *every* night since Holiday Eve?" Robyn asked incredulously as we strolled arm in arm back into the confines of The Manor. As the hour was late, we spoke quietly so as not to disturb.

"Not *every* night," I corrected her "but more often than not." Of the other dream—the one where I was about to go into battle, I mentioned not. After an evening of very unusual experiences being explained, I figured that my credibility had reached its limits for all practical purposes.

"Why did you not mention this while there was still time to be shared in Brighton?" she asked.

"Because until I had left Brighton, I never made the connection that the beautiful girl was you," I explained. "It wasn't until after we were on the way home when a quick nap revealed that most stunning young lady to be you. As it was, when I first laid eyes on you, I had the strangest feeling that we had met before—hence the question of did you recognize me or not?"

"Do you suppose then that I had been dreaming of you as well?" she wondered "and I had never realized having done so."

"That would be one way of explaining it," I offered. "Think back; do you recall experiencing any dreams involving meeting some very handsome stranger at all?"

"All the time," she replied quickly.

"Well, there you have it then. The mystery is solved!" I exclaimed, probably a bit too loudly.

I had never realized just how loudly echoes can fill an empty stone corridor when all else is in silence.

"Dylan?"

"Yes, Robyn."

"The man in those dreams?"

"Yes."

"Um...he wasn't you."

"No?"

"No."

"Oh."

"No...that man was very handsome," she giggled as she dodged away from the retaliation she was certain to be coming her way.

In a night full of newly-discovered truths, we both learned some very important information at that moment. Robyn realized that I can move very quickly—*much* more rapidly than she had anticipated.

I, on the other hand, found out just how ticklish she is.

While the echoes of unrelenting laughter can probably be as loud as any other noise late at night in an empty stone corridor, when one does not care...

Moments later, she stood propped against the corridor walls, red-faced and gasping for air. Too busy to notice, I had learned yet another fact about her—that her fingernails were exceedingly sharp and she knew how to use them! For the next few minutes, I was busy licking the blood from my arm before it could settle upon the corridor floor.

A truce having been declared, it took several moments before we had collected ourselves to the point where we could continue walking.

"I find myself contemplating how much more comfortable our relationship could have been had we both realized back in Brighton some things we now know," she admitted as we came around the corner to the corridor which housed the private chambers for the members of The Staff. Unconsciously slowing our pace as if neither wanted this evening to end, I surprised her when I said I could not agree.

"As I recall, at the time, you were admonishing me for finding humor in funny-shaped clouds," I explained. "Just how well, do you suppose, me telling you that you were the girl of my dreams would have gone over at that point?"

"Not terribly well," she found herself admitting. "I probably would have seen you as just another man with a catchy phrase—the likes of which I have encountered *much* too often during my travels. I doubt if I would have thought enough of you to go anywhere with you. To me—and I know to you as well, trust is something that events in my life has made difficult to easily grant."

"We truly are so much alike," I agreed.

"You could not be more right in your observation," she admitted eventually. "Sometimes I think it would be easier upon us both if it were not so. Perhaps one would be able to follow the lead of the other and bring about an end to this insufferable impasse?"

"And yet, you must agree that there exists an ease between us occurring here this night not seen since that day in Brighton," I answered. My confidence was a bit shaken by the manner in which she indicated our problems could continue unabated.

Running her hand through my hair, she admitted that this has been a most wonderful evening…the best we had ever spent. "Yet does a pleasant evening promise to carry over to the light of day?" she wondered aloud.

"Robyn, since when are there *any* guarantees when it comes to matters of the heart?" I asked as if I had become an expert on such matters.

"Those come with time and trust," she answered readily. "While I believe that we have made solid gains here tonight, does that offer proof of the promise of an extended relationship?" she wondered as she ceased her walk to stare deeply into my eyes.

Remembering the lessons taught to me earlier that day by The Duke, the words *"Robyn, you are wrong"* died upon my lips. Instead, as if The Duke's wisdom finally had worked its way into my thick head, I arrived at what I deemed to be an idea worthy of promise.

"Robyn, perhaps we are not ready for a deep relationship at this point," I said by way of making a statement rather than asking her opinion. Before she could offer any answer, I hurried to explain that without any doubt we were both trying too hard to impress the other for reasons we could not understand and in ways that had not allowed us to be ourselves. "We have impressed each other, and are most certainly attracted to each other; but can we honestly say that we *know* each other?" I asked. I could tell that she was deep in thought while considering the validity of my words. "For my part, I know that I have seen you with unrealistic eyes to such a degree that you could not possibly live up to the perfection which my imagination has claimed," I continued. "I am certain however that will undoubtedly come close," I assured her with a smile upon my face which prompted a chuckle from her.

"Dylan, I believe that you have an amazingly clear understanding of our dilemma," she finally acknowledged. "Fate has decreed that we should meet, and we have readily met those demands. "Does this mean that we run head-long into something neither of us is ready for? I, for one, would like to feel in control of my own life and learn much more about you at a comfortable pace rather than one unsustainable simply to appease what we believe to be our inevitable futures. I desire to see the true Dylan emerge rather than some created character more appropriate to one of his stories. How could we be comfortable with each other if we are not so with ourselves?" she inquired. "Relate to me as me; and I shall do the same with you. Besides," she admitted accompanied by one of her beautiful smiles, "the Dylan that I believe you to be I find that I like very much."

"Then let the gift of your necklace be a pledge of our promise to each other to be ourselves," I announced as I opened the door to her chambers for her. "But I must warn you," I added. "I can do some pretty stupid things when I am being myself!"

"As if I hadn't noticed," she chuckled as we embraced one last time. "Do not worry, however," she assured me as her steps slowly took her inside. "While I may become angry over one of your antics, I am certain I will get over it in time."

She really *doesn't* know me very well, does she?

School Daze

Have you ever had the thought of "*If I was an animal, what kind would I be?*" Almost everyone does at some point. They also usually center on their very best traits, as in "I would be a dog as I am so loyal", or "I must be a bird as I sing so well." Often I like to sit in the town square and watch people while wondering just this question. Some *look* the part of specific animals: quick furtive movements reveal a cat at heart, thin pinched faces with permanent frowns designate a weasel, while a beautiful girl would be a gentle deer with the movements of grace and elegance as she prances through the forest, and…"

Where was I?

Oh yes, matching people to animals.

What animal would I be you ask? In a bit I will tell you, but before I get to that, I need to inform you on what has been occurring here since the Duke, Bryce, and I returned from our little trip to The Channel.

Later the next morning, a group of the Village Elders came to The Manor with the final figures on this year's harvest. As once again the harvest had far exceeded expectations, they wished to discuss with The Duke how to utilize the additional public funds for the betterment of the townsfolk. In Arlington Green, the villagers lived well, we lived well, and the King was happy as he got additional taxes every year.

As word spread how being a member of this town was very advantageous, The Duke was constantly besieged by new families requesting to move in and work for both The Duke *and* themselves. The town was growing—but it was growing too fast. Therefore, it was proposed that any extra money from this year's crop would have to go into getting an additional town well dug, cutting in extra ditches to keep the village dry and clean, as well as clearing some additional land for more crops to be grown.

The Duke realizing the validity of what the Elders had proposed readily agreed to their ideas. Once that business was concluded, he put forth the idea that the timber to be cut down for the land clearing could be used for the construction of a schoolhouse.

The villagers were stunned! These were common folk who had never had the time for—nor even been *allowed* to see—the inside of a school! In order to grow their crops, keep the homes in order, and get the general work completed, they had to rely on their children assisting in doing the tasks. Having a large family assured that necessary work and chores would be done—and yet, the additional mouths to feed required even *more* work by the family in order to feed them all. If these children were to spend valuable time in school, how would all of the chores get done?

Now this was a matter that The Duke had been wrestling with for quite some time. He reasoned that if the children of the village could get a basic education, they would then have the opportunity to be something more than a farmer if they wished. With a better educated workforce, our growing village would have the advantage of attracting new businesses and new ideas, thus creating new revenue for all to share.

"I certainly understand your concerns," he told them, "so what I envision is keeping them in class for only two hours a day for five days a week. That should allow enough time for the chores, don't you agree?"

Now when a Duke says, "Don't you agree", it is rather prudent *for* you to agree. Even this Duke, who was truly a wonderful man, *could* rule with an iron fist if he wished. But that was not his way. The Elders realized this, so to a man they thought it was a marvelous idea and one that could definitely work.

"Good!" exclaimed The Duke. "We do not have a teacher per say here at The Manor, so my Staff will initially handle the teaching responsibilities each to their specialty. As we grow further, a full-time teacher can be added," he said hopefully.

Business was concluded, and the Elders went on their way to sell this amazing new system to a generally stubborn population.

At dinner that evening, The Duke took the opportunity to announce his new plan to us rather stunned members of his Staff. "What I envision is for each of you—meaning Nanny Kaye, Bryce, Robyn, Chef, and myself—to take one day per week for teaching your specialties. This way you will still be able to conclude your responsibilities here as well."

His gaze swept over each of us as he asked, "Don't you agree?"

Remember when I told you that it is prudent to agree when a Duke treats those words as a declaration more than a question? Well, apparently I *didn't* remember, for I naturally had some questions that needed to be answered.

"Sir," I began, much to the concern of everyone else at the table, "what exactly would you be expecting us to teach to these children?"

"An *excellent* question!" The Duke replied to everyone's relief while banging his hand on the table for emphasis. "Each of you has individual talents that, when shared, would benefit the children greatly. Nanny Kaye, you could teach good health habits and well care, while Bryce, your area of expertise would be animal health and measures that could be taken to attempt to increase the village's herds of cattle, goats, and sheep of course. Robyn—as you have decided to accept our invitation and stay on as the newest member of our Staff, you would naturally be teaching music and the arts," he explained to a highly agreeable young lady. "Chef would be excellent at helping them learn which foods can be beneficial and how to prepare those foods in various ways. You would have to oversee their gardens of course to verify the planting of some of this new produce," he added to Chef who was nodding in agreement. "And Dylan, you are going to be responsible for teaching them basic math as well as reading and writing skills."

"And since," he added as an aside, "as you were the only one to endeavor to ask any questions, you have now been promoted to the office of 'School Administrator'; congratulations."

When will I ever learn?

Obviously not now, as I proceeded to ask yet another question. "Sir," I inquired, "just what is a School Administrator to do?"

"Make certain that the new idea of his Duke is a resounding success," he answered very seriously. "You will be responsible for seeing that the children are attending their school time, review what the teacher's lessons are for the coming week and bringing to The Duchess weekly reports on the progress of the endeavor. Not the *status* of the project," he emphasized, "but the *progress*. Do you understand?" he asked as only a Duke could.

"Yes Sir!" I answered. I understood all right—I was in hock to The Duke for Heaven knows *how* long and this was going to be The Duchess's pet project, so I had better deliver!

Once dinner was finished, the five of us 'teachers' retired to the Study where we spent the rest of the evening trying to figure out how to make this new vision of The Duke's successful. We decided that we would each teach on the identical day every week in order to create as little confusion as possible for the children. After that, things got rather complicated!

"Are we going to have all aged children in only one group?" asked Robyn.

"Do we begin our classes at a basic level or ready a more advanced class as well?" Nanny Kaye wanted to know.

"What do we use for *books*?" came from Chef. "I can bring some of my personal recipes, but how will they remember what they are taught if they cannot write it down?"

"Are we going to hold classes all year round, or do we take time off to bring in the harvest or at the Holiday?" was a good question from Bryce.

All of these inquiries were great questions; the only problem was that all of them were directed to *me*! I had no *idea* what to do or how to even go about getting started. This was obviously going to be much more involved than I thought.

Now, I have watched The Duke conduct important affairs for The Manor on numerous occasions, so I have learned three secrets about how to get things done. Item one which I had learned was that when you are unsure—stall. Number two was to delegate responsibility, which is probably how I got this job in the first place, and number three is…well, I can't remember number three right now— but I am sure that it is important.

"Okay, this is what I want done," I found myself saying. "It's getting late, so let's get together tomorrow at lunch. In the meantime, I want each of you to write down an outline of what you are planning to teach and when. This way, maybe we can co-ordinate the lessons and reinforce what the other is doing. Start it basic as none of these children have ever been to any schooling," I reminded them. "Therefore, they will all be starting at the same level. We *may* be able to group more advanced children in the future, but for now, until we know what we are doing, let's keep it simple even for us five."

Was that me? Did I say all that and in a voice that held command and control? I was really impressed! Apparently so was Robyn, for she gave me this look of 'Wow' as she went out the door. Bryce patted me on the back and said, "Nice job Dylan," as *he* left. Chef raised his eyebrows in surprise, while Nanny Kaye told me she was "So excited!"

I must admit that I was excited as well, and mentally made a note to discuss with The Duchess in the morning about acquiring some books and writing materials...because for the life of me I could not remember a word of what I had just said!

I slept little that night as ideas of how I would teach my class and what we wanted to accomplish kept running through my head. I have been to the village on a number of occasions and have always noted the children living there. In many other towns around the country you would find their children thin and with ever-downcast eyes. But in our village, the children generally were better fed and healthier, had laughing darting eyes, and were not afraid of doing a hard day's work. So once the idea of this education process set in, I suspected that they would probably do fairly well.

I had all kinds of ideas by the time the sun came up. Fortunately, as I had some old parchment in my room, I actually wrote them down so this time I would not forget them:

For Robyn- I know that we don't have much time, but we could put on a small show with some traditional singing at Holiday time for the townspeople as well as The Duke and Duchess to enjoy.

For Bryce- Let's try to make sure that there is plenty of feed available for the village animals during the winter even if that means bringing more into The Manor so as to be able to share from our stocks if an emergency arose, for it is easier to increase herds if you don't lose too many to hunger.

For Nanny Kaye- Let's start with trying to keep the children illness free during the winter by teaching them about dirt removal from body parts or however such things are done (not my area of expertise obviously).

For Chef- Take a survey of what is already being grown in the local gardens and fields during various times of the year so as to be able to make suggestions on what can be added to their crops.

And for me- Get the basic numbers and letters into their heads in a way that they can not only understand them but also be able to utilize the concepts in their everyday lives. We were not looking to make scholars of these children. I just wanted them to be able to read at least at basic levels, understand math concepts as they would relate to life in a village, and above all, to assist them in using their minds to form dreams that they never knew could exist for them.

Extra note for Chef- Make excellent lunches for us while we are having these meetings.

I inquired of The Duchess at breakfast if I could have a word with her afterwards. "There are some basic supplies that we are going to need in order to help these children," I told her while we sat having tea after all had departed. "We will need writing tablets, ink and quill, and the teachers will each need ledgers to track how each child is doing as well as form their plans for the lessons."

"How many students do you anticipate?" she asked while peering over the lip of her cup.

I had to stop and think for a moment. "I must admit that I do not have an accurate count as of yet," I replied, "but until I have exact numbers, I roughly figure at least one hundred and fifty or so."

"Count on some sets as extras for Tre and Brandon," she told me. "They are of course going to be attending the school as well."

I began to understand exactly what she was envisioning. "And we will be able to offer your sons additional or advanced lessons here at The Manor in other areas as each of us are going to be responsible for teaching only two hours a day?" I offered.

"Exactly," she replied. "I will be responsible for setting up those studies, so you five just have to concentrate on the school and be available to teach here as needed of course."

I assured her that she would not be disappointed in what manner of education we would be providing for all of the children of Arlington Green.

"I know I won't," she admitted as we rose to leave. "Why do you think that *you* got the Administrator position in the first place?" she asked as she walked out the door, obviously not waiting for an answer nor expecting one.

Did The Duchess actually just give me a compliment?

At the meeting of the five of us teachers that afternoon, I informed them of the progress already made, at which time we hashed out our basic plan for initiating the children's studies.

They all seemed to very interested, especially Robyn who had reached the same idea of the Holiday songfest as me.

I'm sure that I had thought of it first.

We ended the meeting with a target date of two weeks from yesterday to begin our teaching program. Everyone had quite a lot to prepare. I asked Bryce if he had time to take me into the city tomorrow so I could order the supplies. As he was already heading there to arrange for the delivery of additional supplies of straw and feed, he agreed while adding "I would be honored to provide transportation for as important a person as you, Mr. Administrator."

So what was so funny about his statement that had all of them laughing as they left the room?

The idea of creating a code of conduct for the teachers was born in my thoughts, as I could see that they needed guidance in the proper way to treat their immediate superiors!

There are times when I amaze even myself, for when Bryce and I left for the city in the morning, I had a letter signed by The Duke emblazoned with his seal authorizing the bearer to obtain one hundred and sixty writing sets and five ledgers with the charges to be sent to The Manor. I mean, after all—would *you* trust me for that kind of purchase on just my say-so?

You would?

The city is really quite a marvelous place, much bigger than our little village and with anything that you can imagine available. Bryce drove the coach directly to the book-making shop as both he and I can imagine quite a lot. Stepping out of the coach, I began to straighten my appearance when Bryce quipped "Will there be anything else that Your Lordship requires?"

"Only a new groomsman," I grumbled as he left to conduct his business in high spirits indeed.

Once I had entered, the shopkeeper came to the front of his store from working in the back to greet me most cordially. Now this was more like it! I showed him the letter that the Duke had given me; he took one look at the order and asked when we would need it filled by.

"We will require the items in three days," I replied as I wanted extra time after delivery to make sure that all was ready on time.

The shopkeeper became quite flustered. "But…but that is *impossible*!" he stammered. "I can't have that many books ready in that short amount of time!"

All my life I have wanted to be able to do this… always, always, always. Finally, I had my chance! I leaned over the counter, looked the shopkeeper directly in the eyes, and said in my most threatening voice "Do you *really* want me to go back to The Duke and tell him that you refuse to fill his order?"

I must have been good as he melted right in front of me. "Oh no, Sir; I am not telling you that I *won't* fill the order by that time. I am telling you that I *cannot*—no matter how I try!" he informed me as he wiped the sweat forming on his brow with a pocket handkerchief.

"And pray, tell me why not," I continued with my play in spite of the fact that he had called me Sir. "I am certain that The Duke would be *most* interested in whatever excuse given for his request being denied."

I think that I may need to add acting to my resume after this experience.

"Not *denied* Good Sir, for I would never purposely disappoint The Duke," the shopkeeper blubbered. "But creating the type of books that is mentioned in this order takes *time*. The ink, quills, and even the ledgers I have here for you to take with you. But the books? If I work as hard as I can, I can only produce four of those books in an hour with any guarantee of the kind of quality that would satisfy The Duke himself."

That would take nearly a full week to be complete…four days from when I had said they must be ready.

Among the countless things that I am very good (?) at, is the ability to read people. I could tell that this fellow was in earnest and really in a quandary. He wanted to satisfy The Duke's request but could not do the impossible.

That, after all, is *my* job!

"Very well my Good Man," I answered after slight hesitation, "I will go back and tell The Duke that this order shall take more time than he had imagined—but that the reason for this delay is that you had demanded only a quality product would do for so noble a Gentleman as The Duke."

I think that the shopkeeper would have kissed me if I had been close enough. Fortunately, I was not and managed to stay far enough away from him until we had concluded our business.

I was pretty happy with myself as I would have an order of one hundred and sixty of probably the finest writing books in the land delivered to The Manor in plenty of time before our time frame for the school to begin.

I could get the hang of this 'Being a Gentleman of Means' stuff pretty well. I even tried it on Bryce as I went to board the coach waiting for me outside.

"Take me back to The Manor and be right quick about it!" I barked as I opened the carriage door and was about to enter.

Fortunately for me, I only had to walk about a *mile* back home before I found the coach parked on the side of the road with Bryce snoozing inside. Upon his waking, he arched his eyebrows as if wondering if I had learned my lesson. It was a very quiet Dylan that gingerly opened the door of the coach and said nothing for the remainder of the return journey.

To make a long story short—and this is probably the last time that I will ever do that so enjoy the experience—through the hard work of the people of the village, we had our schoolhouse ready the day before classes were scheduled to start. It was very plain building, just a simple one room structure that looked to the five of us teachers and The Duchess like one of the most beautiful buildings that we had ever seen! We moved in all of our supplies including a large piece of slate to be mounted on the back wall for the teachers to use for writing instructions or lessons to the classes. Armed with a list of names of all the children of the village between the ages of six and sixteen, we were ready for the first day of school to begin.

All teacher's lesson plans had been accepted by the School Administrator—meaning me—although I must admit that I may have scrutinize Robyn's plan longer than the others until I got a smack on the head from her.

I *must* look into writing those School Administration by-laws to see if I can get her back in such a way that The Duchess won't feel the need to get involved!

I had selected the school week to begin with Nanny Kaye teaching on Monday, Bryce conducting his classes on Tuesday, myself on Wednesday, followed by Robyn with her musical education course on Thursday, and finishing up the week with Chef on Friday. I wanted to make the first days interesting and exciting for the children as this was going to be a new experience for them. At the same time, I was attempting to keep what could be difficult lesson days followed by lighter days so that extra time could be taken for those children who may have trouble keeping up with the rest of the class.

Besides, it gave me a chance to tell Robyn "You may as well get used to following behind me."

Now I am *positive* that the by-laws will *not* allow for the School Administrator to be kicked in the shins by one of the teachers!

On the first day of school, we introduced ourselves to the children and immediately saw a major problem. None of us had ever realized how large a group of one hundred and fifty children can be, especially when they are all attempting to cram into one tiny room!

We realized that an immediate agenda change was needed to be able to keep any semblance of order and accomplish what we had set out to do. Thus, it was decided that we would divide the group by five. This would mean that on our designated day of the week, each of the teachers would be working full days at the schoolhouse, with a different group of children being taught every two hours. We could get around having only a one-room schoolhouse by holding some of the various classes at different locations. Bryce could teach his students out in the fields and pens where the animals actually lived. Robyn would be happy to teach her group at her favorite spot down by the stream. I would still need to utilize the classroom, but we hurriedly created a removable wall for the center if it should ever be needed. Chef got permission from The Duke—with an assist from The Duchess I would imagine—to be able to have some of his classes held in The Manor kitchen itself. By taking all of these steps, we could carry on until such time as an addition could be added on to the original school house.

Naturally we had our share of problems at first requiring a level-headed individual to come up with rapid solutions, but then that is what a School Administrator does. In this case, he (meaning me) takes all the facts, arranges them into a logical conclusion, and then...goes and asks The Duchess what to do.

Well...it worked!

It has been several weeks now that our school has been operating, and we feel that we are making some real progress with these children. That is, *almost* all of the children. I'll get back to further discussion on the school after telling you about one of our most noteworthy pupils... our young Mr. Barnstable.

I have absolutely no doubt that if he were an animal—and frankly there are some days that I am not so sure he is *not*, he would have to be a plow horse. He is rather large of stature, strong as the proverbial horse, and has an amazing ability of being able to count to ten with his hooves …I mean hands. He *tries* to understand; he really does. But Mr. Theodore Barnstable is one of those folks to whom the word *simple* does not exist.

I am a firm believer in the idea that all people's brains work differently. Some are good at math, for example, while some can excel in understanding science—and still others are talented at song or dance. As individuals, we all have our own ways of looking at things; it just becomes a question some times of do we understand what we are looking at?

With young Mr. Barnstable, I truly begin to wonder if he was even looking at the same things that the rest of us were. He tries to gain an understanding of the lessons that he is taught, especially in writing and math… he really does. And he does have his little victories, as you can almost see a light go on in his head as a concept finally is understood. He does very well in Bryce's classes about animals, and surprisingly can hold his own with Nanny Kaye's health instruction and even Chef's lessons about food and growing things.

But when it comes to communication processes or solid logic principles, it's as if he has run into a brick wall! His mind just does *not* operate that way. In no way does that constitute a flaw in our Mister Barnstable. It just makes him who he is.

And Robyn's attempts with his singing and carrying a tune? Let's just say that he has been 'excused' from that particular part of the program by mandate of the School Administrator. I can only take so much of Robyn's crying and having to go find the animals that have bolted in fear every time he broke out in a tune!

Not having to attend Robyn's classes gives him extra time to get some additional instruction from me. I really have no problem staying late and working with him, for he honestly does try to comprehend. When someone is trying their best and appreciates your help, how can you turn your back on them and just watch them drown in their education? In a strange way, we learn from each other. I have never been a teacher before, so when I have to come up with unconventional ways of getting across to him, it gives me new ideas to use for the rest of the students.

There have been more than a few evenings when I would return to The Manor long after dinner was over due to helping him prepare for some upcoming test or just trying to catch up. He appreciated all the help that I gave him, and he tried hard.

I guess that is all that you can really ask of someone after all.

Being the School Administrator allows me to pretty much do as I want. As Tre and Brandon had already been introduced into the world of education, I often utilized them as tutors to help some of the other children. The boys enjoy helping; I think it gives them a sense of confidence in their own abilities in the process…plus it gave *me* some badly-needed points with The Duchess.

I must admit that watching Tre and Brandon interact with other children from various backgrounds in life is certainly fascinating.

In fact, it was just the other day that Tre came up to me after school had finished for the day. I was sitting at the teacher's desk in the schoolhouse going over next week's lesson planning when he approached me rather sheepishly.

"Dylan," he asked me quietly, "is *thinking* something as bad as actually doing the thing that you had thought of?"

'*Oh this should be easy*' I thought. '*Ethics; just my area of expertise*'! I had him explain his dilemma further.

It appears that a certain young lady in his class, a Judith Smyth, had a knack for getting under his skin. It wasn't anything done on purpose, it was just one of those weird chemistry things where you can't stand someone and you don't really know why.

The solution was an easy one; just switch her into another group and away from Tre.

Dilemma solved!

"So, what were you thinking of doing?" I asked him with the aura of my new-found responsibility about me.

"Well," he began, paused for a few moments, then finally blurted out, "She had really been bothering me lately, so I was going to tell her that if you look far enough down a well, you can actually see the other side of the world! It has rained heavily recently and the wells are full, so all she would get is a little wet when she got a tiny push and fell in."

I realize that one of my main purposes at The Manor is to be somewhat of a mentor to the boys. The position of School Administrator increases my need to be responsible and act as a role model for not only Tre and Brandon, but all of the children of the village. It is an important position that I was given, and I take these responsibilities *very* seriously. It was for moments such as these that I was placed on this earth.

"Tre," I began firmly, "I'm surprised at you! To think that you would actually tell that story to that poor little girl!"

He hung his head in shame.

I was relentless.

"Everybody *knows* that it is the *Fairy World* you see in a well, *not* the other side of the world. Get it right!" I admonished him.

Another moment missed.

Due to the success of our initial efforts, plans have already been drawn up for the extending of the school with some of the funds still available from the harvest. We were hoping for enough to be available to increase the school to three full rooms; all five of us had agreed on that particular vision.

It was *after* that step that life got interesting!

Chef wanted to be able to have a small kitchen included in the plans for his classes. Bryce thought that we should build a small barn and start our own flocks for the children to provide care for. Nanny Kaye knew without a doubt what the larger space needed; a small area where those of the village who had gotten hurt or sick could be cared for.

And Robyn, that most lovely Young Lady with the new dress and necklace...did I tell you that she looks *really* good in that dress? She says that she absolutely *has* to have some musical instruments in order to teach the children how to play.

I was personally hoping for a small stage area where we could put on plays or have the children tell stories or give musical presentations to be part of our new structure, so you can see how if all of our hopes would come to fruition, even three rooms would not be enough.

While the actual decisions would be shared by The Duke and Duchess, everybody seemed to think that I had some special say in the decision-making process. I told them that as the School Administrator, it would be my responsibility to put all of the ideas before both The Duke and Duchess and have them decide on which direction they wished to go. I'm not going to tell the rest of The Staff that I actually have a say in what direction we will be taking.

It's safer this way.

Before we held that meeting however, I went around to several of the businesses and homes in the village to investigate potential alternate plans. Therefore, I was able to approach the Duke and Duchess with a number of suggestions for the three of us to consider.

Increasing our existing school to the three full sized rooms would be a necessity without question, I told them. Once that was decided, I addressed the wants of the individual teachers.

I had made arrangements with one of the local taverns for Chef to hold his classes in their kitchen. What the tavern got in exchange for allowing us the usage of their facilities during slower periods of the day was exciting new foods to add to their menu.

One of the families in the village had lost their father during the past year, creating devastating difficulties to be overcome for their very survival. Instead of building a barn and getting our own animals, why not 'adopt' the family and use our class energy to help care for *their* animals and teach the children real-life experiences while assisting with the welfare of one their neighbors?

With a little clever space usage, we could employ one of the existing rooms as a stage area for the giving of concerts, etc. with the addition of just the hanging of a curtain. This would be especially efficient if we made the wall between room two and three re- moveable so as to increase space during these events.

While Nanny Kaye's idea was an honorable notion, there really was not a need at this time for establishing a center such as she proposed. There were several local women who looked after the health of the sick and injured in the village, so when I had approached them with the idea that perhaps we could arrange for the purchase of some supplies they could utilize in exchange for lessons from them on caring for the sick and injured, they were more than happy to oblige.

So finally we came to Robyn; dear… sweet… Robyn.

I had to admit that with her points to be made, she had a very good argument. In fact, she was *always* giving me a good argument, but that is another story. In this case, she was absolutely right as it *is* very difficult to teach someone how to play music when there are no instruments on which to teach. Musical theory is totally different when taking a bow to a violin and making a sound like a dying rooster!

Buying the instruments that she required was the idea that I was in favor of utilizing any available funds for.

After much discussion among the three of us, it was arranged that we would utilize the tavern for the cooking classes while 'adopting' the village family and purchase a few animals for the benefit of both the classes and the family. Materials would be acquired to make my idea for the moveable stage a reality. We would table Nanny Kay's idea for future reference but make a wagon available in case there was a dire need for anyone to be taken to the city for advanced treatment by a barber-surgeon, while acquiring any needed supplies for the utilization of the healers.

By reaching these compromises, funds for the purchase of a small number of musical instruments from the city would be available. What this fiscal responsibility would also allow for was the possibility of hiring a trained, full-time teacher sometime in the near future. As of now we were still too small of a venture, but if our present success was any indication, we would be continuing to grow rapidly.

I asked The Duke about the possibility that when we were able to afford to hire the full-time teacher, would they take over the duties of the School Administrator as well. He smiled and said that he had the one that he wanted now, but he would keep an open mind in the future.

I think that I just got another compliment!

The results of our meeting was the topic of discussion at the dinner table that evening.

Everyone took the news well, for what they had really desired was the betterment of the children in their classes; those desires were accomplished if not in exactly the manner that they had expected.

Robyn however was thrilled! I even got a hug for what she saw as my assistance in the procurement of the instruments. That was nice...very nice.

Oh, I almost forgot; the answer to the 'what kind of animal would I be?' question.

Well, after receiving my hug from Robyn, I told her how eventually we would be getting a real full-time teacher for the school.

Still excited, she said that she hoped we could find someone who would take the job as seriously as did we five.

In jest, I made the comment that I hoped that we could find a cute girl for the job.

The answer to the original question is…a dead duck!

Pony Tales

Oh, it is a miserable man I am!

Today is the day when The Staff receives their pay for the previous week's efforts. As I am a member of The Staff—although thanks to a certain ship and a dock, I may not be a *paid* member—I am a member none-the-less and am still required to attend. All I can see are smiling faces as I stand in line with the rest of them and watch The Duchess hand them their pay. Yet when it comes to my turn to receive my salary, the same thing happens each and every time. The Duchess raises her head to determine who it is standing before her; when sees that it is me, her hands leave the table to rest upon her lap—at which point she informs The Duke who is sitting next to her notating the transactions in a ledger he keeps that he next person in line is "Dylan Ainsley". The Duke then turns the page to the one with my name on the top, notates the date and the fact that five silver Sovereigns have been paid on the account, then thanks me for my service. I leave the table with empty pockets while being serenaded to the sound of coins clinking in *full* pockets as well as happy laughter from the rest of The Staff as they discuss what they intend to do with their new-found wealth.

I have given up asking The Duke to tell me just how much money I still owe him for Robyn's dress—*and* her necklace—*and* the repairs to fix The Good Luck Charley plus supporting docking structure...which, needless to say, he did not purchase due to its condition. He responds to any inquiry that I make with the same phrase each time. I am so tired of hearing "Five silver Sovereigns less than last week."

So I am penniless due to clothes I do not own, jewelry I do not wear, and a sailing vessel we did not even purchase!

I told you I live a fascinating life!

As a means of ignoring all the happiness I hear in the voices talking about buying this or saving up for that, I escape to the quiet solitude of my room, where once again the same events play out. I have gotten so used to the routine that I have taken to acquiring two new pillows the day before payday to replace the ones that I currently have—which will be punched and kicked until feathers fly!

Lying in my bed while spitting away the occasional goose feather which has landed upon my mouth, I manage to acquire one massive headache while trying to figure out just how much I am going to end up paying The Duke. I keep coming back to the idea that if a simple dress can cost 50 silver Sovereigns, a ship and dock could cost hundreds if not thousands! It did not look good as I figured that I must be into The Duke for a minimum of five years with no pay…and heaven knows how many more times I could mess up during that time and end up owing him even more!

By the next morning, my moping around reached epic proportions to the point that no one could even stand to be around me. At least my poor attitude ended the clever comments I had been receiving—some of which were actually fairly decent I must admit. "Hey Dylan, take a bow," was good. "What's up dock?" may have been a stretch, but my favorite was "Dylan, now I know what shiver me timbers means!"

Try as I might, I could find no one willing to listen as I desperately needed to vent my frustrations. Robyn even went so far as to stuff small pieces of cloth into her ears in an effort to avoid listening to my ravings.

So where would I be able of find an audience that would be willing to stay and listen to me regardless of how badly they wanted to be elsewhere?

Perhaps it was only my imagination, but I could swear I saw panic in the eyes of the horses as I meandered into the stables. Intently pacing back and forth between stall number one all the way to stall number ten—and back again—I began to blister the horse's ears with a terrible tirade! Being familiar with these animal's reactions to my dissertations in the past, I made certain that I kept to the *front end* of my audience.

Eventually, I exhausted the ire within me; and to the everlasting appreciation of our mounts, I found a bale of hay to sit upon as silence reigned once again.

Being unaware of my presence, Bryce came in and began to gently comb the horse's manes. It was a measure of the depth of our friendship that he even remained there once he spied me sitting close by. The gentle motions of his steady combing worked wonders on my frazzled nerves; soon I was relaxed and at peace once again. "You certainly do appear to love your work," I observed.

"Can't say that I look at it *as* work," he replied as he moved on to the mare in the second stall. "Sometimes I think that I like horses more than I do most people," he offered as he continued his long-measured strokes. "Horses don't try to take advantage of each other—or make fun of each other—or any of a number of hurtful things that people often do. If you treat a horse well, you will have a friend for life that will do just about anything for you," he added.

"Can they give me the money to pay back The Duke?" I joked while tossing small pebbles into the dirt. Bryce's response totally surprised me. "In a way, they actually *could*," he told me while continuing his brushing and combing.

I must admit that I was more than a little skeptical. "What do they do?" I asked; "go to the local horse's bank and take out some money?"

I guess I was more than just a *little* skeptical.

Now Bryce is one of the most even-tempered people I have ever known; I don't believe that he even understood the meaning of sarcasm nor read any in my voice, for he just continued with his explanations. "Of course they don't have any money of their *own*, but what they can do is *win* some for you."

The wheels in my brain were beginning to turn as I inquired into this concept with more depth. "How could they possibly win money?" I asked with heightened curiosity. "Do they flip coins like Sir Preston with his two-headed coin?"

"No, nothing like that!" he countered, giving me one of 'those' looks. "What happens is you bet on the horse that you think will win a race—and if he comes in first, then you go collect your winnings."

Now I had heard of something like this before. A number of horses are brought to a tracked area where they race each other…and people make money on the winner. Paying no attention to the fact that the money they won was courtesy of the majority of folks present who had bet incorrectly and just *lost* theirs, I was beginning to be fascinated by this idea.

"So what you are saying is that if I took a little bit of money and went to one of these track racing places, I could win even *more* money?" I inquired. "Just how much more do you think I could win?" I asked hesitantly.

"It's hard to say," he replied while still continuing to run his comb. "It all depends on how lucky you are."

Me…lucky?

Scratch that idea!

"Before I came to Arlington Green, I used to work for one of these track race owners," he informed me further. "While taking care of the horses and keeping the stables clean, I saw many a person walk away with a lot of money that they had not taken there with them," I was told as he finished his combing.

While this sounded great, there were two little tiny problems in that I had no idea where any of these track racing places were nor did I have any money what-so-ever to take to one! Number one problem was solved as Bryce casually mentioned that there was a temporary track racing place that had set-up only several miles down The Capital Road. This was beginning to sound very interesting, except how could I come up with some money to take to the track?

"Um… Bryce—old buddy old pal; I don't suppose…" was as far as I got.

"Sorry Dylan, but I never loan nor borrow money with friends. It's one of the easiest ways to wreck a friendship," he told me with his hand raised in the air to stop me from going any further.

Of course he was absolutely right. But if I could make him like me less, would he *then* loan me some money?

Even I have to admit that was a stupid thought.

So how was I going to get the money that I needed in order to get *more* money that I needed so that I would not need so much money anymore? I was getting very confused, until I spied Sir Preston's horse among the group. Suddenly this did not seem to be such an impossibility, as I think I just *may* have figured out the 'no money' dilemma!

Have you ever flipped coins for money? Have you ever done it with Sir Preston? Try it some time, it can be *very* rewarding. I won't bore you with a play-by-play account of the coin flips and how I maneuvered him into making the wrong call each time, but when we had finished, I had 20 brand new silver Sovereigns!

Hurrying over to where Bryce was sitting and watching the world go by, I asked him if he would like to show me what makes a racing horse different from a cart horse—which he said he was more than happy to do. So with a pocket full of jingling coins, we were off to the races!

Let me stop right here. You may be thinking that if I took those 20 silver Sovereigns and gave them to The Duke, I would owe him that much less and be better off, right? After all that would be the smart thing to do, right?

Have you ever known me to do the smart thing? That concept doesn't appear very often in my natural way of being me.

Saying goodbye to our fellow Staff Members—I made certain that I stayed away from either The Duke or The Duchess with this money in my pockets—Bryce and I left for the day to go to the track racing establishment.

As we approached the track, I began to understand just what an incredible place it was! There were dozens and dozens of horses of all breeds and colors waiting for their chance to race. Hundreds of people, all dressed better than I was (a hint maybe?) were crowded around the white fence that encircled the dirt track. Wave upon wave of cheers roared out from the crowd as the current group of horses rounded the corner and headed for the 'finish line'.

Aren't I getting good at this whole racing thing?

Bryce walked me through the lines of horses tethered and waiting their turns to run. He pointed out the various breeds and what made them different such as height, size, and some other things that I was paying no attention to as I was only there to win some money.

We watched as a string of horses was led off to take their turn. "Hey Bryce," I asked innocently, "which one do you think will win out of that group of horses?"

"That's easy!" he replied. "The black mare obviously has the edge." How he came up with his answer I had no idea, but I wanted to take advantage of his expertise. "So how would a fellow go about…what did you call it… *betting* on that horse?"

Bryce showed me some tents set up away from the track itself. All I had to do is go inside and tell them which horse I wanted to put my money on while turning over however much I wanted to bet…at which point they would give me a slip of paper. If my horse won, I would turn the slip back in and collect my winnings.

"So how much would I win if I bet, oh…say one silver coin?" I wanted to know.

"It all depends on the odds," he explained "If there are ten horses running in a race, only one can win, right? Now, like I told you, in this particular group the black mare is the strongest, so she will possibly win the race. I said *possibly* because many factors need to be considered such as closing speed, position, and so forth."

I must admit that I had *no* clue what he was talking about.

"Some people would like to bet on that horse, called the *favorite*, because it has the best chance of winning," he said while patting the flank of the nearest horse. "Because of that, if their chosen horse wins, they do not get very much money. It is when one of the *other* horses wins unexpectedly that the payoff is the best."

"But how do they decide on how much you could win?" I asked, anxiously fingering the Sovereigns in my pocket as I listened to the roar of the crowd as the previous race had just concluded.

"By what the odds of winning are for that horse," he answered. "The less of a chance a horse has to win a race, the higher the odds are set so that some bettors will take more of a risk and wager their money on it. If that horse can actually *win*, they get more money because they took that risk. Those horses are called 'long shots' and that is why this is called *gambling* and not *winning*!" he said, indicating what he thought of betting on horses in the first place.

I must admit that I felt like I should walk away right then and there with my newly-found wealth, but I was desperate! After all, I had started the day with only 1 coin and now I had twenty jingling in my greedy little pockets, hadn't I? What if I could win enough to clear my debt to The Duke? Against my better judgment, I started walking towards the red-topped tent which Bryce had indicated was where the bets would be placed. I got into a line that slowly wound its way inside and ended at a shady-looking character sitting behind a table.

"What's your pleasure, Mate?" he asked indifferently without even bothering to look me in the face.

I had been watching the people in line who had placed their bets before me, so I sort of had an idea of what to do. Using the insight that Bryce had given me as to the inevitable winner, I told him "Give me two Sovereigns on the black mare to win." I figured that until I got the hang of this, I would not bet all of my money at once.

"Fine," replied 'Mr. Shady', waiting impatiently with quill in hand. "What's its name?"

Taken aback by his question, I blurted out "Name? What do you mean what's its name? How should I know?"

Bryce had never mentioned anything about names!

The people around me began to snicker—unless they were behind me waiting to place their own bets—in which case they began to register their impatience.

Trying once again by utilizing all of the information I had available, I told him "It's the big black mare…that's the one I want."

By now, the snickering had turned to laughter.

"Boy, all of the horses have names," said Mr. Shady as he finally bothered to look up. "You have to give me a name so I can write it on your ticket."

I sheepishly got out of line without making a bet. I made my way trackside, where the race was about to begin. Anxious bettors with slips of paper clutched tightly in their fists crowded around the fence line. The horses were led up to a line marked in the dirt, their riders small men and boys with various colored streamers attached to their arms to designate their particular horse in the field. The crowd's excitement was building to a frenzy until the sound of the smacking of a bell signified the beginning of the race—and then they were off!

These were eight of the fastest horses I had ever seen as they flashed around the corners and headed for another line at the end of the track. Sure enough, just as Bryce had predicted, the black mare won! If I had just known its name, I would have had an extra four silver Sovereigns as I found out that it paid 2 to 1.

This was *way* too easy!

I remembered what Bryce had told me about the long shots making you more money if they won, and worked some more odds in my head. If a horse had 10 to 1 odds, and I bet my two coins on it to win, I would get an additional twenty Sovereigns in my pockets if it won! At this rate, I would be able to pay the Duke back very soon…perhaps even today.

Amidst the happy laughter of those folks who had just won, I went up to a board where a man that looked like Mr. Shady's twin brother was writing down numbers. "This is the odds board," he told me in reply to my inquiry. "As more bets are made, the odds change—and I write them down on this-here board so the bettors can make their decisions."

Oh, this really was getting too easy! I would wait by that board with the rest of the quiet losers and when the highest odds came out, I would go and place a bet on that horse. At this rate, I would need a wheelbarrow to take my winnings home!

The next race was about to begin and the final odds were posted. A horse named 'Old Nag' was set at 15 to 1. I just knew that in this horse I had a winner as it *was* named after Robyn, so how could I lose? I quickly figured out the payoff if I bet four of my Sovereigns, and came up with a whopping sixty in winnings! Why that was almost the entire cost of Robyn's dress; this was *definitely* fate.

I went back up to Mr. Shady Number One sitting behind his desk and with the swagger of an old hand said "Give me four on 'Old Nag' to win." I handed over the money and took my piece of paper down towards the track.

Looking back on it all, I can tell you *exactly* when this master plan started to go wrong…it was the moment when I asked Bryce about racing horses!

I saw the horse named 'Old Nag' being led up to the starting line. This was a horse? If it was, it was the first one that I had ever seen the size of a large dog, blind in one eye, and with one leg shorter than the others. There was no way that this horse…this *thing* …was going to win!

As fast as I could run, I sped back to the betting tent! Not waiting in any 'line', I pushed and shoved my way right up in front of Mr. Shady. "Wait!" I yelled, while doing my best to catch my breath. "There's been a mistake—I want my money back!"

Have you ever seen a cat smile at a mouse when it knows the mouse is his next meal? That was the expression I saw upon Mr. Shady's face as he introduce me to 'Mr. Big and Ugly'! Not only did they not give me my money back, I was immediately thrown out of the tent to land in the dirt amidst dozens of torn-up losing betting slips.

Things were not going exactly as I had planned. Of course 'Old Nag' did not win…it never even finished the race! With four of my original Sovereigns now gone, I had to turn things around fast!

Brushing myself off, I sauntered over to check the odds board. The best that was available for this race was 8 to 1 on a horse named 'Good Luck'. I figured that if I took eight of the coins I had left—which was double my original bet—and won at 8 to 1 odds, I would gain sixty four into my pockets! I went back into the betting tent and got into a different line—where I got to meet '*Mrs*. Shady'. I bet the eight Sovereigns, took my paper slip, and left for the track being careful so as not to bump into Mr. Big and Ugly again.

We all know what a nose is, right? Some may be bigger than others or may have been broken once or twice, but we all have them. Well—horses have them, too. I know this to be true because Good Luck lost by just that... a nose! The 64 silver Sovereigns that I had expected to win vanished in a puff of smoke, along with my betting ticket into the closest fire.

Standing dejectedly with the rest of the losers, I did some quick reckoning. I originally had twenty coins in my pocket; minus the twelve that I had already lost left a measly eight silver Sovereigns—along with one rather angry Dylan! At this point, all I wanted to do was win my original money back and go on home. I was beginning to learn my lesson...but only just *beginning*.

I went back to the odds board, but with a different strategy this time. I would put all of the money I had left—my eight silver Sovereigns—on the horse favored to win the next race. I would not make a *lot* of money, but if I continued to follow this strategy, at least I would get back to where I had started.

The odds were only two to one on the favorite 'Fire Breeze' when I stood before Mr. Shady while placing my fateful bet of "eight on Fire Breeze to win." Confident that I had done the right thing this time, when I left the tent, curiosity led me back to the odds board. According to the board, the long-shot in the upcoming race was a horse named 'Ocean Biscuit' at 16 to 1.

Ocean Biscuit? Who would be dumb enough to put money down on a horse named Ocean Biscuit?

The race had just started when I got down to the track. Sure enough, Fire Breeze was out in front. Around the first turn he began to open up an even larger lead! At the second turn, he was a full three horses long ahead of his nearest rival—which surprisingly happened to be Ocean Biscuit. Each stride of Fire Breeze's mighty legs made the gap between him and Ocean Biscuit greater and the distance to the finish line that much closer!

Closer and closer to the finish came Fire Breeze…my heart was pumping rapidly as I found myself jumping up and down while screaming at the top of my lungs "Go Fire Breeze…GO!" Just a few more seconds, and I win! Just a few more seconds…

They say that before today it had never ever happened in the entire *history* of Racing Horses! They would be talking about it for years to come, I had heard. 'Amazing' others called it!

The object of all the excited discussion was a bee…a small, simple little bee. This bee had made its way under Fire Breeze's saddle, and just as he approached the finish line, the bee had decided to sting Fire Breeze right in the butt! The horse stopped dead in its tracks, which flung his rider off and straight over the finish line! The *rider* won the race, but without the horse under him—which is of course against the rules. That is why Fire Breeze did not win…and thus allowed Ocean Biscuit to win at the incredible odds of 16 to 1!

I thought that I was going to be sick.! Not only did I not win more money to help pay off The Duke, but I had lost every last silver coin that I had!

Having finally had enough, I stumbled about looking for Bryce as all I wanted to do was go back to The Manor and hide in my comfortable bed as quickly as I could get there. In my search for him, I passed person after person counting their winnings or laughing at the ending of the last race.

I was devastated!

I finally found Bryce right where he should be, looking over the horses and admiring the champions. He could tell that it was time to leave by the look on my face. Without a word being spoken, we began the long trek back home.

I kept hearing a strange noise as we walked; sort of like a 'jingle… clink…jingle'. I looked around, but only Bryce and I were to be seen. I asked Bryce if he was hearing the noise, too.

"Yes, I am," he answered cheerfully. "What you are hearing is the sound of the money in my pockets which I won by betting on Ocean Biscuit. Ten silver Sovereigns and at 16 to 1—I can barely *walk* I am weighed down so heavily! Hey Dylan, do you think that maybe I should have gotten a wheelbarrow?" he asked while smiling happily.

Seasonings for the Holidays

Having lived the life of a vagabond wanderer for years before claiming Arlington Green as my home, I have roamed throughout the Realm experiencing events both marvelous and terrible to behold. I have certainly visited many wonderful places and met some very interesting folks, yet I can state with complete conviction that there is absolutely nothing better than being at The Manor of Arlington Green during the time of the Holidays.

A light covering of snow blankets the ground, the cold of the winter makes the fire seem warmer and cheerier, and if you hide behind the big barrel outside of stall number three you won't be seen and you can pop Robyn with a snowball!

Seriously, there is no place where I would rather be and at no other time of the year. It may sound quite odd, but when the snow covers the ground and life appears to slow down, this is the busiest time of the entire year for us.

Have you ever tried to decorate an entire Manor? They are fairly big after all! There's the entire inside to do with the halls and the walls, then get to the outdoors including the stalls. Of course there are the parties to prepare, the friendship to share, and the big barrel outside of stall number three to beware!

Hey, that was pretty good. I think I'll write it down for later.

It is at this time of the year that the kindness of The Duke and Duchess becomes evident for all to enjoy. You see, several years ago they established the tradition of preparing an enormous amount of food, then taking those meals down to the village to share with the people who will not be having such a nice meal to celebrate with on their own...or possibly not have any at all for that matter! I hear that this used to be a major task until they found our marvelous cook Chef. Now it's Chef who does all the planning, ordering, oversees the food preparation, and handles all of the minor glitches to insure that they never become major problems.

It's not like the people in the village don't know where their magnificent bounty comes from every year. But both The Duke and Duchess, in spite of the fact that they are Nobility, are humble folks at heart and want no credit or thanks for their generosity. Therefore, it is left to us Staff members to quietly deliver the goods every Holiday in the early morning hours while the villagers are still asleep. To accomplish this, there are some special tasks that need to be done every year such as greasing the axel of the cart so that it does not squeak during our journey or getting out special coverings to put over the cart so that the warmth of the food stays in and our fingers stay out! We even tie branches of trees onto the back of the cart to cover our tracks from The Manor to the Village and back again.

Everyone knows, but no one says. Like I have told you before, The Duke and Duchess are truly marvelous people.

Last, but certainly not least on the list of things to do for the Holiday, are the gifts to get for each other. Nothing major you understand, just small items to remind us all that it is the time of the year for giving and that we are thinking of each other and appreciate one another. I asked Robyn if that nice dress I got her for the incident in the stables would count as her gift from me, but she just looked at me and went to get me a hat as she said my brain must be freezing.

As you will recall, I was so deep in debt to The Duke that I was working basically for free and was completely broke! I had approached him several times with the idea of asking to borrow a little more money to get some presents for everyone, but he must have known what I was about as the words "Don't even think about it!" escaped his lips before I could ask. "Besides, it's the thought of the giving that counts, not the gift," he added.

"But Sir," I countered, "if it truly is the *thought* of the giving that counts and not the gift, could we not just *think* that I paid you back the money that I owe you?"

I don't think that I had ever heard The Duke laugh as long and as hearty in my life as he did just then.

So, in addition to helping with all that was going on in The Manor, I had to really use my wits to come up with ideas for presents for everyone.

Now, The Duke had been completely right when he said that it was the thought of the gift that was important. I came to realize just how wise of a man he was when it dawned on me that by really thinking about the individual, I could come up with something that was special to that person in spite of having no money at all to spend. For instance, I went into the stables and found a new nail that could be used to keep on a horse's shoe—I would give that to Sir Preston so that he could replace the one missing from the shoe of his horse to keep it from hobbling. I would give Chef a note that said I would clean up the kitchen for him after evening meal for a week. Simple little things like that would carry special meaning to the recipient because they were created with special thought and consideration.

I was able to come up with something for everyone except for—Robyn! What could I possibly give to her that would be special, very meaningful, and cost no money? I had already tried that new dress thing and that didn't work, so I knew that she was looking forward to something—but what?

I would have to come up with a solution in between all of my tasks, for in addition to being the assistant decorator, I was also the assistant cart preparer, assistant cook, and the person responsible for doing anything that The Duke thought up and wanted done.

What made this all worse was that every time that I passed Robyn in the hallway, she would get this big smile on her face that told me she had gotten me something really special and couldn't wait to give it to me. No matter how much I thought, I could not figure out what to get for her!

All preparations went into high gear as it was now the day before the Holiday, and we had an enormous amount of food to prepare. All types of different dishes required particular attention such as roast goose, plum puddings, cookies of all varieties, roasted potatoes, cooked vegetables, and …all of a sudden I am *so* hungry! Deliveries were coming into The Manor all day long needing to be accepted, brought into the kitchen, and begin to get prepared. Everyone with the exception of The Duke and his family were busy; for this was our present to them every year. We would handle all of the work needing to be done for the traditional Village feasting. It was the best gift that we could give to the two people whom we admired so much and wanted to do something very special for.

Would you believe that originally this had been my idea?

You would?

Well it wasn't, but thanks for believing it anyway.

In between bringing in barrels of apples to be peeled and cored, I would try to think of what to get for Robyn. While helping to roast the potatoes, all I could concentrate on was that I still had not gotten her anything. I was absentmindedly overseeing to the roasting of a goose and still had come up with nothing. Chef came by, took a look, and said that my goose was cooked.

No truer words had ever been spoken!

Time was flying…literally…as Chef threw his sand timer at Sir Preston to keep him from tasting the plum pudding. To Robyn's horror, all throughout the day as we worked we would break out into off-key renditions of cheerful Holiday songs. We rarely finished them, however, as bouts of hilarious laughter mixed with wonderful aromas reigned as the champions of our kitchen.

Darkness had set in for the evening by the time all of the preparations were complete. We loaded the wagon with all of the goodies, blanketed it with the special covering to keep warm things warm, cold things cold, and our fingers to ourselves. We did not have long to wait until we were ready to begin our trip to the village.

This short break gave me some time to wrestle with my dilemma. What if I gave Robyn a note promising her that I would not throw any more snowballs at her from behind the big barrel at stall number three? No, that wouldn't work, for by now she knew me too well to believe in such fallacy and would realize that I would just move over to behind the woodpile and still throw the snowballs.

I went outside to try to come up with some inspiration. Taking a moment to recall the events of last year's Holiday Eve, I raised my gaze to the heavens and offered a heart-felt thank you. It was chilly but not too cold, with just a hint of a coming snow in the air. When all was still, you could hear the sound of faint singing coming up from the village below. For the night before the Holiday, everything was beautiful. No, it was better than beautiful—it was perfect!

Except for not having come any closer to solving my problem that is.

That would have to wait as it was now time to get going down to the village with the cart laden with the villager's Holiday feasts. Bryce drove the wagon, with me sitting next to him on the seat. This is the only time of the year that I get to sit up front on the seat of the wagon; the food has a better chance of arriving at its destination intact if I am up front. Chef sits in the back of the wagon surrounded by his creations like a mother hen amidst her chicks, while Sir Preston accompanies us on his warhorse just in case of—actually I'm not sure *why* he accompanies us—he just does.

Silently we crept through the now-sleeping village. The aroma of wood smoke got lost in the stiffening breeze as we quietly made our way towards the end of the village and the houses furthest away from The Manor. Without a sound, Bryce stopped the wagon. He and I stepped to the rear of the wagon where Chef would hand us entire meals which we would quietly take up to the front door of the nearby homes, taking care to assure that it would be the Villagers themselves and not their dogs or pets that would be enjoying this wonderful bounty. When we had gotten all of the houses in that area, we would get back on the wagon and quietly go a little farther up the road to some more houses, repeating the process over and over again until we were finished.

Sometime during the night, it had started to snow. I really can't remember when, as I was using my full brain capacity to make certain that I made no slip-ups with my deliveries, as well as figure out how to swipe an extra apple pie from in front of Chef's very nose! It was a kind of game we played, for he made certain he had an extra pie on the cart; this in fact was my traditional Holiday present from him and he enjoyed immensely watching how I was trying to be clever. He saw when I got the pie, but still let me think I was getting the better of him. Like I said, it was a very special time of year.

We arrived back at the gates of The Manor just as the sky began to brighten. There would be no sun that day as the snow was falling, yet in the hearts of everyone in The Manor and in the Village down below, the rosy glow of such a wonderful Holiday experience could melt the deepest of snows from the harshest of blizzards! We got the horses bedded down, and once Bryce had presented them with their traditional treat of honey-covered apples, we tiredly made our way into The Manor and its warmth.

Now, we may do things a bit differently than most, but it's *our* way and that's what matters.

At this point, everyone is exhausted from days and days of non-stop preparing and delivering, so we gather to indulge in our large Holiday feast in the morning when we return and then go to sleep until evening when we open our presents. We do this because it is that magical time in the morning when our hearts are most filled with the warmth of what we have just accomplished, making it the perfect time for all to gather together and enjoy the happiness of the moment coupled with the most wonderful meal as could ever be imagined. Having the table set and prepared as we went to make our run of food to the village was Robyn and Kaye's job, and this year they created a setting more festive and beautiful than ever before.

Now, I am a Storyteller and a pretty good one if I say so myself. Yet as I looked around the table, seeing everyone's tired yet smiling eyes, their expressions of pure enjoyment as tasty dishes one after the other are experienced, and actually *feel* the warmth and love flowing from each and every heart filling the very air that we breathed—if I could even *begin* to help you sense what this Holiday time was like for all of us sitting around that table, then and *only then* would I consider myself worthy of the title of Storyteller.

Once our appetites were finally sated and our stomachs happily and totally full, exhaustion naturally sets in as we slowly drag ourselves off to a well-deserved sleep.

Now we were all children once ourselves, and some of us still are if you believe a certain young lady, so we can all understand that two children plus presents unopened equals no sleep for anyone. It is for this very reason that The Duchess came up with a wonderful holiday tradition of her own. Every year, the feast begins with a toast from The Duke and Duchess to all of us for our continued health and happiness now and in the coming year. It is a beautiful sentiment to which we all raise our glasses and take a drink. The boys are of course encouraged to join us in this tradition. But what they do not know is that several days before the feast, The Duchess

makes a trip to the local chemist for a wonderful white powder which, when mixed into a small glass at just the right amount, will give you two sleeping boys within an hour. That is her present to each of us because…
WE ARE GOING TO GET SOME SLEEP!

The first one of us to waken later on in the day rings the traditional holiday bell which is meant to waken the rest of us to slowly and tiredly trudge our way to the ballroom, where we throw the traditional balls of smelly stockings at the person who rang the bell and woke us up in the first place!

I love this time of year, and while I love presents as much as anyone, I am proud to say that I never…ever…have rung that stupid bell. As we are all awake at that point, we enjoy warm punch and cookies while the opening of the presents begins.

The presents!

My heart jumped into my throat as I realized that I had gotten so caught up in the moment that I had completely forgotten that I had not gotten Robyn *any* present.

I was doomed!

Gathered in the large Library, beautifully decorated for the season, The Duke and Duchess stand amidst the pile of presents while the rest of us sit about on the floor like small children filled with excitement. The Duke would pick up a gaily-wrapped box or parcel, call out the name of the person who it was for and from whom, at which point that person would come up to receive the present. Name after name was called, presents were exchanged, and the large pile of gifts was getting smaller by the minute, when The Duke announced, "To Dylan…from Robyn."

Getting to my feet, I tried to keep from looking over in her direction as my sense of guilt was eating me up! Of course I could not help sneaking a quick glance out of the corner of my eye. I believe we could have extinguished the fire, for she was smiling so warmly that it was not needed any longer to keep the cold out of this room. I sheepishly walked slowly up to The Duke and accepted the package wrapped in bright red ribbon—Robyn's favorite color. My fingers moved as if by themselves as I unwrapped her beautiful gift.

It was the most handsome leather-bound writing book I had ever seen—including ink and quill! Slowly, I opened the cover. On the front page were written the words: *To Dylan, so that he can create stories that will be enjoyed by many for years to come*. And at the bottom—signed by her own hand, were the words…*Love Robyn*.

It was absolutely beautiful; never had I received so wonderful a present that carried with it such meaning. Tears were welling in my eyes as I suddenly hated myself as I was about to terribly disappoint the girl who had just opened her heart to me by giving me the most thoughtful present I had ever received and even signed it with *LOVE!*

I made my way back to my spot among the group clutching my book tightly in my hands. I happened to look over at Robyn, who was still flashing me the happiest of smiles mixed with tears of joy at the depth of my response! She had even worn the dress that I had bought her coupled with her new bright shinny necklace.

I hung my head and slowly sat down in my place, my eyes fixed upon a spot on the cold stone floor as I could look her in the eyes no longer or share in her beautiful smile.

What had originally been a large pile of presents was rapidly dwindling into just a few more left to open.

Emotionally I was reaching a place where I had never been before. How could a person be so *happy* and yet feel *so* miserable? My head was literally swimming when I heard…what?

Did the Duke really just announce "To Robyn from Dylan?"

Robyn got to her feet and was walking towards The Duke, so *something* must have happened. But how could this be?

"Dylan, would you come up here as well?" he asked, motioning for me to join them.

The Duchess rose and stood by The Duke's side while I, as if in a dream, found myself walking towards The Duke and the eagerly waiting Robyn. Her eyes were alive with curiosity, happiness, and I think maybe just a little concern at what I had concocted. I came to stand next to her as The Duke handed her a brightly wrapped red box. Slowly, and with trembling hands, she unwrapped the red paper until another smaller box was revealed. This box was a *deep* red as it was made of velvet, not paper. Robyn shot me a quick look of total surprise as she spied the new box. I really... *really* hope that I hadn't had the same look on *my* face at that moment, for I was completely confused while doing my best to hide that fact from her.

Opening the velvet box revealed a small sheet of paper edged with a red band. There was writing on the paper, which read: *Would you please accompany me into the Sitting Room?* signed in my name. It didn't look much like my signature, but at that point it didn't really matter. The Duke and Duchess turned and began walking toward the Sitting Room; Robyn and I slowly followed.

The large innately carved wooden doors to the Sitting Room slowly opened. Inside, a nice warm fire was blazing. Next to the fire, a table had been set with small portions of all of the foods that we had enjoyed earlier during this morning's feast. A bottle of one of The Duke's finest wines perched on the table with two glasses nearby. There were no chairs at the table, just a nice comfortable love seat facing the fire.

What *was* all this? I hadn't done any of this. On my *best* day I couldn't come up with anything like *this*!

What was going on?

The Duke motioned Robyn into the room. Before I could enter, he stopped me and placed a small card in my hand. I read what was written on the card but could not believe my eyes! It read: *To Dylan from The Duke and Duchess: for all that you do for us…and to us. Happy Holiday.*

Can you believe this? I was penniless—could not get Robyn *anything* for the Holiday—The Duke had even refused to lend me some money for a present—and yet here was this most *marvelous* present that had been cooked up for me by The Duchess and Himself!

I looked up from reading the card, as I am certain that my face was expressing both gratitude as well as confusion.

"You do many good things for us, Dylan," spoke The Duchess quietly. "And the Duke isn't the *only* one who is very good at paybacks," she added with a smile.

Never would I be able to make up to the two of them what they had just done for me—and especially for Robyn! But I don't think I would have to. I believe that the look in my eyes as I quietly thanked them both was enough for them.

I walked into the Sitting Room as the doors slowly closed behind me. I sat down next to Robyn in the seat, trying as best to keep over to my side, but a love seat was built for two people to get to know each other better. As of yet there had been no speaking as we just sat staring into the fire. I don't know if we even knew what to say to each other; I could see that she was about as nervous as I.

If she noticed the shaking of my hand while I opened the bottle of wine and poured each of us a glass, she made no mention. I handed her the wine—I *might* have touched her hand for a moment or two longer than was needed—raised my glass to hers and quietly toasted "Happy Holiday."

The food was excellent and the wine was hearty. It must have been the magic of the Holiday, or possibly the warmth of the fire, or perhaps the sound of the silently falling snow outside—but whatever the reason, we found ourselves relaxed in each others company not found since the Festival of Music, making meaningful small talk as we *never* had been able to before. More food brought on more wine followed by yet more conversation. She was even laughing at my humor…and she *meant* it!

This was the most marvelous event that I had ever experienced! I'd like to think that she felt the same, and I think that she may have for she reached over and kissed me. "Thank you for this marvelous gift," she said to me as I became lost in her eyes; "for I don't believe that I have *ever* enjoyed myself more."

We had completed eating and set back into the comfort of the love seat when I felt something under the seat. Reaching under the cushion, I brought out yet another small red velvet box. Robyn looked at me in delight; I looked back at her in confusion as we opened the box together.

Inside we found two golden chains each sporting a tiny golden fish. One was obviously meant for each of us; we put the chains on each other and settled back into the comfort of the cushions.

The Duke is very VERY good at paybacks.

The fire was starting to die out and a chill was beginning to spread; soon we found ourselves in each others arms for warmth.

Outside, the sound of the light wind blowing the fresh coat of snow around our little world made what was left of the fire seem cozy, but not as comfortable as the warmth of Robyn in my arms. We just sat together, staring into the fire, speaking not a word.

It was together in each others arms that we fell asleep that night.

Listening to the sound of Robyn's gentle breathing in my ear as she slept in my arms, my last thought before I drifted into one of the most restful sleeps that I had ever enjoyed was that this was undoubtedly the *greatest* Holiday I had ever enjoyed and could possibly be the start of a wonderful New Year.

Yeah buddy!

Construction Destruction

While I am tempted to say that I have only two kinds of luck—bad luck or no luck at all, I have to be honest with myself. When I stop and look at where I am in life, I realize I have the perfect job for me. My benefactors The Duke and Duchess are wonderful to work for and with and I am surrounded by people who make Storytelling easy by being—shall I say—*quirky*.

And I even used to have a wonderful girlfriend named Robyn. I say used to, for it appears that she has found someone else who captures her interest!

I know that I am jumping ahead of myself and should start at the beginning, but every time I think of that craven knave who stole my woman, I...

There, I feel better now.

Where was I? Oh yes, that *$*>^%!!!

Sorry about that.

Not really.

As you will recall, Tre and his Father had taken our idea of building a mill to the townsfolk for approval. The money for the project was arranged by The Duke and placed in a separate account. I think that they called it an 'as grow' account—or something similar—to be utilized by The Duchess to pay for the costs of building and operating said mill. We had already begun the process of clearing the land for stones and downing trees for the lumber needed to construct our mill.

But we still needed a builder to bring it all together.

The Duke, once again accompanied by Tre, went to The Capital to interview members of the Builder's Guild in order to obtain the best one they could get and afford. As luck would have it, they settled on one fellow, a Mr. Martin Sinclair, who came highly recommended. It was arranged that he would reside in The Manor with the rest of us until construction of the mill was completed.

When they both returned and informed us at dinner how this 'Martin' would be arriving in three days to begin the project, we all were sort of like 'okay…great…whatever'. Yet I couldn't help but notice how one person among us seemed to be trying to conceal their discomfort. That person was, of all people, the lovely and beautiful Robyn. After dinner as I was walking her back to her room, I inquired as to whether she knew this gentleman due to her response during dinner.

She was surprised that I had noticed her reaction. "Yes, I know Martin," she replied hesitantly. "I knew him when I was younger, but we have not seen each other for some years now."

As a Storyteller without peer—or so I tell everyone, one of the skills I have is to be able to observe people and situations closely. We arrived at her door, gave each other a quick kiss, and parted for the evening. As I walked down to my own room, what I had observed in Robyn was deeply disturbing, for when she had talked about this Martin, tears had begun to form in her eyes. Obviously there was a considerable connection shared between them…and I was going to find out what it was!

The next two days flew by as I was very busy with my duties at school as well as being a temporary foreman overseeing the workers gathering the materials for the building of the mill. Thus I was unable to spend much time with Robyn other than at dinner. In spite of this limited time together,

I could not help but notice an increasing sense of anticipation about her. Whoever this Martin Sinclair was, there definitely had been a *strong* bond between the two of them.

I must admit that I was surprised by my own reaction to this knowledge. I was incredibly bothered by this man—and I had not even met him. He could be a man of honor and integrity, someone to know and even call friend; so why was I so apprehensive about his arrival? I finally decided I would clear my thoughts and feelings in order to give this Martin a chance when I met him—the low-bellied slimy snake!

It was known around the village how the new builder had arrived at The Manor earlier that afternoon, and apparently would be introduced to the rest of The Staff later that evening at dinner. I had a strange feeling this was one meal that I would remember for a long time to come.

The sun was beginning to set as I made my way back to The Manor. I could not help but notice that the western sky had turned a shade of red… an omen perhaps? For red was Robyn's favorite color—as well as the color of blood!

The question was, would it be this Martin's blood—or my own?

An extra setting had been placed at the table when I arrived early for dinner. I took my usual place between the seats of Robyn and Bryce and waited…patiently.

Yep, just waiting…just sitting around doing nothing…patiently!

One by one, everyone began filling in for the evening meal. When we were all present, The Duke and Duchess entered. We stood for their arrival, yet the two of them remained standing after motioning for us to take our seats, the signal they wished to make the inevitable announcement.

He introduced one Martin Sinclair as the Mill Builder who would be staying in The Manor throughout its construction. The door to the dining hall opened, and in walked…

I guessed him to be in his late twenties, with a full head of blondish hair and no beard. He had what women would call 'ruggedly handsome' features I suppose. His clothes were not fashionable but new and clean. Flashing a warm smile to all, he approached the table.

I was glad I had decided to hold judgment on him until we had an opportunity to meet. Now we had met, and I hated him immediately!

We went around the table, introducing ourselves and explaining what our duties were at The Manor. When it came to Robyn's turn, you could detect discomfort from both parties when they did not look at each other while Robyn gave a curt explanation of her responsibilities.

My turn came next. I was short and sharp in my introduction, and his reaction to my explanation did not help matters.

"So this is the Dylan whom I have heard about in the city," he proclaimed smiling openly. "Your reputation as an excellent Teller-of-Tales proceeds you, Sir. It is indeed a pleasure to meet you." It was a warm and honest statement. Normally, I would be looking at The Duke as if to say 'see…did you hear that…he said excellent'. But in this case, all I could do is stare back at him and mumble a short thank you and welcome to our Manor.

Noticing how Robyn's hands were trembling. I reached out my own hand to hold hers. Initially she looked embarrassed, but her expression immediately turned to a warm smile of appreciation as we continued to hold hands until the food was served.

Light conversation was prominent during the meal, most of it directed to our new guest. Martin would politely answer questions from those around the table, describing buildings and locations which he had overseen the construction of. Everyone had questions to ask—except both Robyn and I. We ate in silence, our eyes hardly leaving our plates.

I was determined after dinner to inquire of Robyn what had been the connection between her and this Martin. Unfortunately, I could only watch as she left the room slowly as if under a great weight, for The Duke required me to remain afterwards to discuss progress on the procurement of materials for the mill with both himself and Martin.

I informed them of the amount of stone and lumber which was already available. I even offered to give Martin a tour of the fields and forest where our materials were being gathered. I was especially anxious to show him the site at the river where the mill was to be built; people have been known to 'slip' accidentally into the river after all!

The meeting ended, and I realized how it was too late to search out Robyn and find out what this secret relationship was which the two of them had shared.

It was a very uneasy Dylan who tried to sleep that night. I was experiencing an emotion which I had never had regarding a woman before. I was jealous of some other fellow, and it was not a good feeling.

The next morning, I gave 'Marvelous Martin' his tour of the town and our facilities. He was impressed by our progress in so short a time. When we approached the river, he viewed our proposed site for the mill with his trained eye. He asked me questions about the river, such as how high does it get in spring and how low in the summer. He agreed with my initial assessment that this was a good location in which to build as the ground was firm and a constant flow of water should be available throughout the year. He was praising me for my choices, but all I heard was the hissing of a snake.

He had just taken my favorite fishing spot. It does not matter that I had picked out the site originally—it was all *his* fault.

Oh yeah…and he had upset my girlfriend, too!

I found myself hating him even more.

It was time for my class to be taught, so I bid him farewell and headed off towards the schoolhouse. Robyn's group was just finishing up as I arrived, so we passed each other in the doorway.

"I need to talk to you," I told her as we dodged the children entering for their lessons.

I could not help but notice that she appeared distressed. "Not right now," she said as if distracted. I got a quick "Later…okay?" for an answer as she hurried outside and off towards The Manor.

Four times my class had to remind me where I was, for my mind certainly was not there. Realizing how I was doing them no good, I gave them all a quick quiz; Was it day or night? Everyone who got it right could leave early for the day. After three tries for young Mr. Barnstable, the room was finally empty. I closed the door for the night and hurried to The Manor.

Arriving short of breath, I looked all over for Robyn. She was not in her room, nor in any of the common rooms where she normally could be found. Chef had not seen her, nor had Bryce or Sir Preston. Finally, Nanny Kaye said rather quizzically "Have you tried out in the garden?"

Walking outside, I heard muffled talking around the corner by the roses. Quiet as a dead mouse in a cat's mouth, I crept around the corner. I must admit, I must have looked humorous tip-toeing in the grass.

Of course, the talking was going on between Robyn and Martin. I could not get close enough to hear what was being said, but I certainly could read the gestures they were making. Robyn's movements were measured and closed, as if she was protecting her inner self from hurt or pain. Martin on the other hand was gesturing heavily with arms opening widely and hands placed on his heart! He was talking louder and more often than her, as she would only reply in short bursts.

So how would you read this scenario? Probably the same as I did; old lovers brought together once again by fate. My hunch appeared to be correct as Martin reached out to take Robyn in his arms. She remained stiff and aloof, until with a great bout of crying, she melted in his arms.

I had seen enough.

Looking back on it now, I am proud of what I did next. I did not confront those two right there and then, nor did I go borrow some of Sir Preston's sharper objects to get a good view of Martin's innards!

No, instead I took a walk to my favorite fishing spot, dropped my line, and had a good think. I remembered times such as Holiday night—or when the two of us worked together on musical lyrics and song until I could almost hear the sound of her voice—as well as the way she looked in the new dress which I had bought her.

Did I tell you that she looked really REALLY good in that dress?

I thought of what our relationship was, for after all we were not betrothed or anything formal. Of course there was a mutual interest — how could she help it, poor child? But busy schedules had kept what could have been a budding relationship from growing into...what?

I decided to write down a list of all the positives a relationship with her involved as well as any negatives. I reached for the writing tablet which never left my side and opened it only to see the sentiment she had written when she gave it to me as a Holiday present.

'Love' was the closing—or was it a hope of a beginning?

I finished my list in a very short time.

For the first time, I was honest with myself, or at least I think so. A long list of positives was balanced by only a single notation in the space saved for the negatives. That notation read 'Martin'.

So what was I going to do about it? Or more important, what was I *willing* to do—and give for that matter? What did I truly want? I searched long and hard into the very depths of my eternal soul.

It took all of about a second to come to the realization that I knew what I wanted— Robyn!

But what had I shown her regarding my feelings? We had our hand holding and some kissing, but I never remember telling her what I felt for her. Perhaps because until this moment, I really did not know what it was that I felt?

But I certainly knew now!

Straight as an arrow shot, I sped back towards The Manor. I was determined to confront those two and profess my feelings for my Fair Lady and let the chips fall where they may!

Besides, it was almost dinner time anyway.

Once again I got to the table first and sat waiting...patiently. Yep, just me by myself...waiting calmly. I looked down in surprise to see my napkin getting twisted tightly in my hands. I must have been calmly thinking that the napkin was Martin's neck. But to my credit, I *was* wringing it *patiently*!

My worst nightmare was proven correct, for Robyn and Martin both entered the dining room at the same time, talking openly—and smiling.

Smiling!

At each other!

I couldn't help but notice that she also was not wearing the gold necklace with the small red stone which I had bought for her. I couldn't remember the last time she had left it off. Maybe that should have told me something. That's me, good old Dylan, Master of the Obvious.

Surprisingly, she still sat down next to me at the table. 'Marvelous Martin' even moved her chair out for her and pushed it in towards the table once she had sat. My hands were trembling under the table as I twisted the piece of linen into a permanent pretzel!

She looked over at me. My face must have betrayed my feelings, for she knew something was bothering me. Her eyes got very inquisitive wanting to know what was wrong, but I answered her not. I was trying to control my actions as there were sharp knives on the table and 'Mr. Wonderful' was seated directly across from me.

At that moment, The Duke and Duchess entered the room. We all stood until they were seated, then commenced to sit ourselves to begin the dinner. Not to be outdone, I quickly grabbed the back of Robyn's chair in an effort to help her be seated just as 'Mr. Marvelous' had done. Apparently, he was much better at it than I, for in trying to push in an astonished Robyn, I ended up banging her knee into a table leg and almost tipping her over.

My actions got mixed reviews from those at the table. Bryce and Chef almost broke out in laughter. Sir Preston pretended he did not see anything—at least I think he was pretending. Nanny Kaye's face went from complete surprise to something akin to a smile of relief. I could not see any reaction from The Duke or Duchess other than a small faint nod passed between them.

I plopped down in my chair, more than a bit embarrassed.

Robyn, however, never even broke into a grin. She was smiling a nice kind smile as she thanked me for the effort. She even whispered to me "You never did *that* before."

I was tempted to reply, "I never killed your old boyfriend before either," but managed to keep my tongue quiet for once.

Dinner was pleasant I suppose, with small talk wrapped around a fine meal of roasted pig.

The Duke asked Martin about his impressions of our plans for the mill. I heard not a word, for I was too busy imagining Martin's face on that of the roasted pig! It wasn't until I heard my name mentioned that I paid any attention to their conversation at all.

Martin was telling The Duke how our site was perfect and that the materials were being gathered to the point where actual construction could begin within the week. He was saying how I had done a very creditable job in preparing the next phase. He stopped at that point, as if waiting for an acknowledgement from me for his gesture, but all I could do was mutter under my breath where I would like to put one of our pieces of lumber!

Apparently Robyn overheard my blurb, for I got from her both a look of reproach as well as a new bruise on my leg.

As my voice was in gear preparing to yell in pain, I controlled my outburst into a belated "Thank you for your kindness," and went about massaging my throbbing leg. I got another dirty look from her and went about the business of eating my dinner in silence.

Once all of the courses of the meal were complete, I was startled to see Robyn rise from the table asking for everyone's attention as she had an announcement to make.

I was too late! I would never get a chance to tell her the truth of how I felt about her now. She would of course tell everyone about a renewed relationship between her and 'Mr. Dead Pig Face'. A sudden thought came to me: What if she would leave The Manor when the mill was done?

I may never see her again!

Now I am famous for doing things without thinking, and at that moment I kept my reputation intact, for I jumped up away from the table like my behind was on fire! I startled Robyn, who completely lost her train of thought as she dodged my falling chair. Before she had an opportunity to get back to her thoughts, I reached for her hand and proceeded to pour into what became known famously around The Manor as 'Dylan's Terrific Tirade'.

Looking deeply into her eyes, and in words which came from somewhere within me, I began to tell her exactly how I felt about her! I was determined to have her hear what I was about, and if she still wanted to make her announcement afterwards, well... at least she would do it while knowing my heart.

I told her of all the ways which she makes me smile. I referred to every time that I saw her as 'the feeling you get in springtime when you see the first blossoms of the new year'. I said that I had been a fool (which apparently took no one by surprise) not to have realized all of this earlier. I totally opened my heart when I said I must have been afraid to express what was truly inside me, but the thought of losing her was even more terrifying. For all I knew, we were all alone in that room, for I had neither eyes nor thoughts for anyone else. I ended up my soliloquy by looking directly into those beautiful eyes…and telling her how I loved her! No jokes—no back-pedals—just an honest expression of what I wanted her—no, *needed* her to know.

"You can go and make your announcement now if you wish," I told her as I flopped down in my chair, both physically and mentally exhausted.

The room was filled with a stunned silence. I sheepishly peered around the table to see expressions of shock, happiness, even some satisfaction; yet from no one at that table did I experience any feelings of laughter or belittlement at my professing of what I truly was about.

I had tested the impressions of everyone there except Robyn and 'Mr. Wonderbritches'. I slowly turned toward the Lady whom I had called 'the light of my life' (did I really say that?) to gauge her reaction.

I believe that the phrase 'total shock' would be an appropriate choice in gauging her reaction. Her eyes were wide, her gaze directly upon the empty plate before her. She was breathing heavier than normal; had I made her physically ill with my transgressions? She closed her eyes for a moment, reopened them slowly, and turned to face me.

I had no way of knowing what expression showed on my face at that moment. Was it hope which could be read upon my countenance—or maybe relief at finally saying what I had truly felt—or could it be worry that all I had expressed had fallen on deaf ears with her eyes only for Mr. Dead Pig Face?

I was not too certain about the condition of her ears and eyes, but I had absolutely no doubt about her lips as she threw herself into my arms and we proceeded to share a kiss which would last for ages!

How long it lasted, I had no way of knowing. Was I still breathing? I did not care.

We slowly parted gazing into each others eyes to the sound of raucous clapping filling the room as everyone was standing and cheering. I looked over across the table and was shocked and amazed to see 'Mr. Nice Try but You Lost Her' probably clapping the loudest.

I slid the sharp knife out of my sleeve as apparently I would not need it after all.

When quiet had been restored, The Duke called for one of his finest wines in order to toast the event. "For it is not every day when a lady is so lucky to have *two* men enter her life," he announced happily.

Um...say what?

Two men? Seems to me that is one too many.

Looks of confusion were shared about the table until Robyn stood once again and finally got to make her announcement. It appears I had been right—sort of. There had indeed been a relationship between both Robyn and Martin in the past...one of sister to brother! A falling out several years ago had left them both unable to relate to the other until the ice finally thawed in the garden this afternoon. It must have been just that meeting which I had spied from my hiding place.

Brother? Mr. Dead Pig Face was her brother?

Then I didn't have to worry about losing her?

I didn't have to face the rest of my life without her.

I did not have to make a fool of myself in front of all of these people!

I began to feel more than a bit embarrassed at what for me was a breakthrough moment of finally acknowledging my true emotions. That thought was instantly replaced as the quite respectable Mr. Martin Sinclair, Builder Extraordinaire, came over to embrace us both. A cacophony of sound was all I could hear as one after another of the occupants of the table came over to shake my hand or give Robyn a hug. Sir Preston started to do the hug thing to me, but I stopped him in short order and gave up my hand to shake instead.

The rest of the evening is still a blur. I can remember raising a glass of the most marvelous wine a number of times to toast Robyn's and my good fortune. It sounded sort of funny, this 'Robyn and I', for that is truly what we had just become.

I was only Dylan no more.

I do recall walking Robyn back to her room arm-in-arm after the festivities had ended. And while a gentleman does not discuss such things about the one whom he loves, the old days of a quick kiss on the cheek were gone.

Long gone!

Yeah Buddy.

Beautiful Music Can Be a Noteworthy Experience

Me...me...me...can't...can't...can't...sing...sing...sing. Tis true, I *can't* carry a tune with a shovel. The good thing is that I don't *have* to; there is a certain Young Lady here who handles that nicely, and now she even has some competition as the Festival of Music was being held this year in the fields surrounding The Manor of Arlington Green. Hundreds and hundreds of musicians, singers, songwriters, jugglers, and lovers of music were flocking to The Festival, bringing lots and lots of coins into the pockets of the local inns and taverns. Tents of all sizes and colors were being set up on the green fields in preparation of the week-long festivities. Wagons full of musical instruments, all kinds of food, and boisterous and melodious singers were plodding along the roadways toward their own personal brush with destiny. For to win any of the categories at The Festival could assure an individual singer or group of at least temporary fame and future work in taverns and fairs. For the very lucky who are extraordinarily talented, performing in Manors for nobility and their guests during banquets can be very rewarding indeed. The pressure was enormous on the entrants—and thus on a certain talented Storyteller.

Fortunately, The Festival was being run by an experienced crew of folks, so I was not responsible for it in any way even though it was being held on our home turf.

That is, once I had gotten out the proper decorations for The Manor walls, helped to prepare the open rooms in The Manor for the Noble guests who would be entertained within, gotten our class in animal husbandry to clean up all of the 'meadow muffins' that the cows had left behind in the fields, and completed the most impossible mission that I had ever undertaken; I had to get Robyn ready for the event.

Now Robyn is undoubtedly one of the most talented singers and musicians that I have ever seen or heard; the only problem is that she does *not* believe it. She knows she can sing and play, but she sees herself as little better than average. No matter how often I tell her that she is tremendous, she gives me that look that indicates "You have to say that."

Naturally, being the quasi-host for The Festival, our Manor could not have our very own Songstress not enter the lists; at least that is what I told her as I helped her complete her entry notice. I am very proud of my Little Songbird and want to have others enjoy the pleasure that her voice brings.

So I have all of that working against me, plus the fact that our school choir will be entered in the event as well.

There's no nervousness here—of course not.

There's no pressure here—hah, not here.

And there's no feeling here in my *fingers* after Robyn was finished nervously squeezing my hand as side by side we stood while she signed her name into the lists!

Together we picked out the musical number that our little school choir would sing. But when it came to her own entry, nothing that I suggested was good enough. Even the songs that we had written together would not work for her for this special event.

I casually said that if we could not find a work that she could use, I would have to write her a brand-new song.

Caught!

I guess it seemed fair to her that if she had to enter this contest, then I would have to come up with some new gem for her to perform.

I tried to lighten up her tension with the following hastily concocted ditty:

"Gardner... Gardner... why work you harder?
Please tell me what is the scoop?
The garden grows in rows and rows
Must be from all of that cow..."

That's when she hit me in the head!

"If you can't take this situation seriously, then maybe I won't sing at all!" she scolded me as her nervousness showed through.

"Yeah, well if you keep hitting me in the head, then I won't be able to think about any new songs!"

That's what I *should* have said. Instead, all I said was "I will have you a beautiful song in plenty of time for you to prepare for your performance."

It's not that I am scared of her or anything you understand, it's just that I am being supportive.

Yeah, that's it—*supportive*.

Now, we had been working with our school choir for quite a long time in advance of this event, so they should be fairly ready. The beautiful thing about a bunch of small children doing a song is that nobody expects them to be perfect because they *are* small children. Cute yes, but perfect no. And come on, who does cute better than me?

In this particular instance, I must admit that Robyn came up with the theme. We had chosen a traditional song that welcomes in the spring after a long cold winter, so to highlight the effort, she had all of the girls outfitted as tiny flowers while the boys were costumed as birds and small forest creatures. They may not be the best singing choir, but they were undoubtedly the most darling.

Feeling fairly confident that we have prepared them as best we could, my focus next fell upon the choir mistress. She was putting so much of her effort into readying *their* production, it seemed that she was ignoring her own entry. I needed to come up with a song quickly before she could claim that she did not have enough time to practice and thus withdraw from The Festival.

For her song to be done well, the subject had to be something that was important to her. While the notes themselves were always right and on-key any time she performed, it was when she sang from the heart that her melodies were filled with such emotion they were quite capable of bringing tears to one's eyes. Therefore, I would need a quiet ballad for her rather than an up-tempo folk song. The words were mine, but the music and tune would be hers. That is, after all, how a good team works.

I took some time away from whatever The Duchess could find for me to do and went to Robyn's and my favorite spot down by the pond. I needed to get away from everything and *everybody* to concentrate, and what better place than here to do that—now that my fishing spot was gone. Tens upon tens of subjects flashed through my mind, yet nothing fit. For a song is like a story; it just happens to be told to music, and a good story begins with an idea and then just flows until the tale is complete.

I looked all around me for inspiration yet could not come up with any beginning. There were trees, singing birds, a gentle breeze, and a small babbling brook feeding into our little pond; all in all, it was a wonderful place to be, but nothing came to mind as far as a song. It was truly a beautiful place—it was our place—*our* place.

As if a dam had been removed from a river, once the thought entered my mind it began to build up speed until, as if a wave upon the shore it crested, broke upon the riverbank, and was still. My fingers flew across the paper as with quill in hand I tried to re-capture the words and emotions that had just filled my head—and my heart.

I completed the song with a flourish, stopped, and then re-read what I had put down on paper. Had I captured just what I was looking for? What words needed to be replaced for either a stronger emphasis or a more loving touch? I tweaked that song numerous times, then tweaked it some more. Strangely, every time I changed anything about the work, the next time I read it, I changed it back to the original version. Finally, I figured out that as the very first effort had come directly from my heart, I would stay with that one after all.

The song now was complete; the main question that remained was how it would be accepted by Robyn to be sung in front of hundreds of people who were all critics of music and its contents?

Rushing back home to show the song to Robyn as quickly as possible, I finally found her in The Study working on one of the costumes for the choir. She could tell that I was excited; she has learned to read me rather well. Maybe it was the fact that I had run into the room, or that I was fighting for breath while yelling "I got it!"; some *small* hint must have given me away.

I handed her what I had written down. I watched her face for any hint of what she was feeling as she read the text of the song. Even if it was good, and she felt right about it, she would still have to take it and set it to music.

A smile came to her face slowly, her eyes dancing as she finished reading the text. She closed her eyes; I could tell that she was trying to set the words to appropriate music in her mind.

Apparently I had done well, as, smiling broadly, she threw her arms around my neck and gave me a kiss that seemed to last for hours. "Tis a beautiful song," she said finally with smiling eyes, "one that I will be proud to sing. But there is only one problem—you have forgotten to include the name of the song with the words."

I whispered the name into her ear.

She looked deep into my eyes as if trying to read down into my very soul. "I will work on it today and sing it for you to critique as soon as it is ready," she offered happily.

I slowly shook my head no. "There is only one place for this song to originate and that is from your heart," I told her. "Therefore, you must sing it from the heart. If I should hear only pieces of it at a time with changes in tune or words, the power of the message would diminish. I will hear it proudly when you perform at The Festival," I told her as I tenderly kissed her forehead. "And perhaps," I added, "never again. For when perfection is reached, any other effort would steal from the memory of that most perfect moment. And that is what I know you will deliver," I told her with confidence.

The happy recipient of numerous kisses of gratitude, I left to give her the chance to work on the piece. Sneaking along the corridor so as not to be spotted and put back to work, I could feel my fishing pole calling me. Unfortunately, I bumped into The Duchess as I rounded the corner, and her voice spoke volumes louder than any fishing pole ever could, as I was given a list of new errands to run. Somewhere in the cool clear waters of the river, a fish that would have ended this day on a platter waved its fins not knowing that its life had been saved by no less than a Duchess!

Notices were posted about town and into the cities listing various people and groups that would be performing for The Festival. Some very prominent names of groups as well as individual talents were posted on those bills. And right in the middle of them all was the name of my own Lady Fair. I took down a copy to keep for a souvenir. I was not going to show Robyn the paper just yet; she certainly did not need any extra pressure placed upon her.

In order to help our little singers work the nervousness out of their systems before *their* performance, we had arranged to have them sing their song before The Duke and Duchess the day before The Festival began. As you can imagine, the children were nervous—Robyn and I, on the other hand, were frantic! We set up what was supposed to be a small stage in the Ballroom, complete with a curtain. We wanted to re-create similarities that they would experience the next day so as to get them relaxed and looking forward to performing. We got all of the children in their places as the curtain slowly rose.

The Duke and The Duchess were seated while Chef, Nanny Kaye, and Bryce stood behind them, all faces brimming with large open smiles. I looked over at the children and immediately knew we had a problem. To a child, their eyes were as big as they could get, their faces blank as if they had not only forgotten their song but also the reason for being there in the first place! Robyn and I tried to get the children's attention from the sides where we were positioned, but to no avail. This was not good and would just add to Robyn's nervousness and unease for her own presentation.

Being a Teller-of-Tales, I was used to being in front of people on a regular basis. This, however, was a totally new experience for the children. It was one thing to perform for their own families as we had done the week prior, but now they were terrified to be in front of The Duke and Duchess! I could only imagine that they would have same reaction when they looked out into an audience of several hundred strangers.

It was obvious that they would need a leader on stage to break them out of their panic and into the performance. Neither Robyn nor I had any influence on them from the sideline, so being the inspiration that I am—some would spell that I-d-i-o-t— I leaped onto the stage amidst the startled children. I spun a short tale to explain the idea for the song, making several small jokes in the process. I could see the children start to relax and chuckle. I threatened to sing the song if they would not—*that* moved them into action. Robyn began playing her mandolin, the choir started in on cue, and the performance went beautifully.

The Duke and The Duchess were very moved and impressed when the song had finished. Not only did they clap their hands for several minutes, but they rose up and personally spoke to each and every child as they shook their hands in congratulations. Nanny Kaye huddled amongst the children offering praises while Chef brought out special treats for them to enjoy. I had noticed that Bryce was not among the group yet gave it no more thought. The children were beaming—now they were ready for tomorrow.

We got the children out of their costumes and sent them off back home with as much praises and accolades as we could produce.

Robyn was smiling from the wings; our eyes met and she mouthed a quiet 'thank you' to me. I was truly feeling good until I turned around to face—both The Duke and Duchess themselves!

A Teller-of-Tales has to be able to read their audience in order to know in which direction the story needs to go to get the maximum enjoyment for their efforts. I had gotten very good at this if I do say so myself, and the look that I was getting from the both of them spelled doom for old Dylan.

The Duke was trying hard not to laugh but could not conceal it very well. The Duchess, on the other hand, was totally enraptured in what she was about to say. Obviously they had been talking and plotting, and I don't think that I was going to enjoy this at all.

"A *marvelous* performance," The Duchess began; "the children were just *wonderful*! And those costumes? Adorable—just adorable." She turned to Robyn and said, "You should be very proud of yourself My Dear; you have done a truly wonderful job."

Then she turned to me.

"And what costume will *you* be wearing tomorrow when you are on stage with the children?" she asked me casually.

Um...what?

"None, My Lady, for I will not *be* on stage with them for the performance," I answered, knowing full well that it would not end there.

It was The Duke's turn now to dangle old Dylan over an open fire. "They obviously *need* a leader with them in case they respond the same way tomorrow," he began, doing his best to keep a straight face. "They recognize you and follow your lead. I really believe that you need to be on stage, don't you agree, My Dear?"

This last one was directed at Robyn. She could barely keep her face from splitting she was smiling so widely. "Oh, no doubt Sir," she responded cheerfully. "Do you think that he would make a good geranium or perhaps a cute little squirrel with a big bushy tail?"

Somebody was going to pay for this.

The trouble is, that somebody was going to be me!

I tried to wiggle out of this as quickly as possible. "I do agree that my being on the stage *could* be advantageous, but to wear some sort of costume in the process? It seems to me that such an exhibition would do naught but diminish the impression of the children themselves on their audience," I reasoned hopefully.

Good effort—no chance! The three of them were enjoying this *much* too well.

"Not diminish, but more like *enhance*...don 't you agree?" The Duchess asked of her other two conspirators.

At this point, as they were suffering from a severe bout of chuckling, the best that The Duke and Robyn could do was nod their heads in agreement.

"Then it is settled," The Duchess announced firmly in such a manner as to let me know that any attempt at dissuading her would be met with dire consequences. "And to assure that it is ready on time, I *personally* will make your costume for you."

There goes my best excuse.

"May I ask Your Ladyship just what this costume will consist of?" I inquired with concern etched upon my face.

"Yes," she said as she exited the room with The Duke arm in arm; "you may ask."

And then they were gone.

I could see that Robyn was just waiting for me to start venting. But what I really saw was the relaxation and lack of nervousness that she was exhibiting for the first time in days. For her sake, I let it go.

"Hey, maybe she will make me a pile of cow poop so I can lay down for the whole performance," I offered lightly.

That did it—she exploded into laughter! "Well it would be appropriate if they do a poor job," she said laughing so hard she could barely catch her breath. The empty room echoed long with the sound of our giggling and joy.

She left to go and work on her song, while I left to see if I could sneak a peek at what The Duchess was preparing.

As I cautiously rounded the corner outside of their suite, I found myself staring directly into the eyes of…Sir Preston.

"Sorry Lad," he said, "but I am under orders that you are not to enter this door under any circumstances—per The Duchess herself."

Ah, the chess game was on!

I left as if in defeat, but I was *far* from done in. As soon as I got out of his vision, I ran for the outside courtyard. If I climbed the large tree in the center of the yard, maybe I would be able to spy on what was being prepared.

Check!

She had placed Bryce at the base of the tree with instructions that I was not allowed to do any climbing. I thought that I detected a bit of a grin on his generally dour face as he wiped his hands on a rag yet paid the matter no attention.

My move again!

From personal experience, I knew that if one got on top of the barn roof, one could drop a snowball down a certain young lady's back; maybe that vantage point could give me a view to solve this mystery.

Aha. She had not thought of this one! I cautiously began climbing the backside of the barn, hand after hand, foot after foot until I was just about to the top when I noticed that the barn roof appeared to be coated in some substance—some very *slippery* substance!

I scrambled to gain a hold, but I was slipping fast and could not slow up the effects of the fall. I was going down and could not stop myself.

I glanced down at the ground in anticipation of where I would land, and—funny, I didn't remember those little brown piles in the grass before.

Oh no, she would not!

Like an arrow launched at a bull's eye, I landed flat on my back directly in the center of the piles.

Oh yes, she did!

A familiar odor wafted about me as I lay there trying to catch my breath. Was it horse or cow…I could not be sure for my heading was spinning wildly from my fall.

Not that it mattered much of course.

I became aware of two people looking down at me as I lay. I got my eyes to focus to find that it was The Duke and The Duchess standing above me. The Duke was openly chuckling, while The Duchess appeared solemn.

Only one word was spoken; it happened to be offered by The Duchess. In that one word the gauntlet was thrown and the war was on! I promised myself while lying there on the ground amidst the aromatic brown mounds that retaliation would be swift and definite.

"Checkmate!" was all that she said.

Dylan Enjoys a Fling

I must have scrubbed and scrubbed until I was raw, yet somehow the scent of those piles of poop just would not go away. I began to think that maybe they were etched into my memory for all time.

Yeah, like I'm really going to forget!

Oh, sweet revenge be mine.

Unfortunately, any notions of immediate retaliation would have to wait, for today was the opening of The Festival of Music. Not a problem, for paybacks are best done when the party receiving said activity has forgotten the need for such action. I could wait—and I *would* plan!

In the meantime, I was rather busy. We had been fortunate in that our school choir would be performing their number on the very first day. Sometimes it is best to do what you are concerned about as soon as possible rather than have to wait around and think about your nervousness. Robyn, on the other hand, would not be doing her solo until the following afternoon. This gave the both of us a chance to be there to get the children ready and encourage their efforts while still guaranteeing Robyn enough time to practice—and panic!

What this also did was keep The Duchess from having much time to prepare this 'costume' that I was to wear for the performance. There was no way could she finish anything *that* quickly, I reasoned.

As usual I was right, but as is also usual, I was wrong at the same time. This ability of mine is indeed an art form that few individuals are *capable* of yet alone so darned good at. For The Duchess was not able to complete a costume in such a short time by herself, which is why she recruited Nanny Kaye to help her finish the task.

I took one look at what was being held up for my inspection and ratcheted up the payback scale to the power of infinity! I was not going to be a flower. I wouldn't even have to be one of the small woodland animals. No, good old Dylan was not to be *that* lucky.

Now, there are few songs sweeter in nature than that of the bluebird; but I ask you, have you ever seen one that is six feet tall? If you can picture me encased in cloth the color of several different hues of blue, with big brown bird feet and a cute little tail that would swish every time I moved, you can begin to understand.

The children loved it of course, while Robyn could not stop laughing—and I don't believe that she had ever really tried. Naturally, The Duchess played it *perfectly*; she was discussing with Nanny Kaye if they should have let it out further in the stomach area. Nanny, in all seriousness, offered that if I would watch what I ate, that would not be necessary—at least by *next* year's Festival.

Bring it on people; I can take it, and I certainly will dish it out!

At least it took the tension away from the children before the performance and seemed to calm down a previously anxious Robyn.

We carried our costumes to the staging area prior to our scheduled time. The children were in awe as we passed many varied stalls and stands containing foods, sweets, and items that they could only imagine in their dreams. Every color of the rainbow and then some were displayed throughout the fair. Fire-breathers and acrobats performed their acts of daring and skill as we passed by, the children's eyes wide in amazement! The sound of music was everywhere; I must admit that I found myself being as dazzled as the children were by the display.

Maybe Robyn is right, and I am just a big child?

No, not a big child—a big dang bluebird! I was praying that any colleagues of mine would not be in the audience during our performance, for I do have a reputation to uphold after all.

Yes, I do!

The sound of clapping and whistling erupted from in front of the stage curtain behind which we were waiting nervously as the group before us completed their song. They did very well; we would have to be on top of our game. The heck with worrying about this bluebird nonsense. I would rise to the occasion and be the leader that these kids required.

The previous group began to troop past us where we waited to go on next. They had done well but did not have any special outfits upon them.

Advantage us.

The announcer introduced us to the crowd, the clapping began, and the curtain rose.

I could not believe the size of the crowd that awaited us in front of that stage. *Hundreds* of anxious faces were turned towards us; the entire town plus many other folks must have turned out to see us perform.

Eyes wide open—feet frozen in fear—throat as dry as a desert—and that was just me.

I could only imagine how the kids were responding to their first view of the large amount of people anxiously waiting to hear them sing.

Actually, it was pretty much the same for them. They had taken their correct places on the stage when they began to spot parents, siblings, and friends out in the sea of faces; *that* pretty much did them in. I looked over at Robyn, ready at her mandolin to begin the music for our song. She looked back at me as if *pleading* for me to do something to break this silence and fear that was beginning to become noticeable.

I broke the silence all right.

A sudden sneeze escaped me, which caused me to move slightly and trip over my big old bird feet! The crowd howled in delight, the kids broke through their sense of terror to even laugh, while Robyn almost dropped her mandolin in surprise. In trying to get back up, I knocked over a small pail of whitewash, which naturally looked like I had left a bird dropping right in the middle of the stage.

There wasn't a dry eye in the audience, they were laughing so hard. But it had worked, for the kids were laughing and relaxed; we were almost ready to begin.

Very, *very* carefully I walked up to the front of the stage. The crowd was beginning to calm down in anticipation of the performance beginning.

I made the following announcement: "On behalf of the children, Robyn, and myself, we would like to thank you for that warm welcome. We believe that music is something to be enjoyed at all levels. We try to keep our program fun for the kids, hence the little display just now."

Yeah...right.

"They have worked very hard, and we are very proud of each and every one of them. Ladies and gentlemen, may I present the Arlington Green Children's Choir."

Robyn hit the beginning note, the kids began their song—at first a little tentative, then growing in strength with every new note. I couldn't tell you if we were on stage for 30 seconds or 30 hours. But what I can tell you is that the crowd stood and clapped for over two minutes when they had finished.

I put out my hand for Robyn to join us; she was beaming with pride and just a bit teary from happiness. The kids were all smiles, proud and delighted.

What a wonderful experience!

My hand hurt from all of the shaking that I received from the parents of those children after we had left the stage. Hugs were given, backs were patted, and unfortunately a few jokes were offered. "Hey Dylan, maybe you should change the name of the group to 'The Birds' ha ha."

What a dumb idea! What kind of name was that for a singing group?

Item one had gone very well; now it was time to put my full attention on item two.

As we walked out of the stage area, I asked Robyn how her song was going.

"Well, the tune is very good—it's the words that still need working on," she replied, twisting out of my range with a light-hearted laugh. Now this was my Little Songbird, with her heart light as a feather.

Her heart—my brain—we make such a perfect match.

She left to go work on her effort, so I took to walking about The Festival taking in all the sights and sounds—and oh those smells! I found myself sampling various dishes that I had not tasted since my arrival at The Manor and was happy to discover Chef out there doing the same. I managed to direct him towards some of my favorites in the hopes that we would be enjoying them during one of our future dinners.

The Festival of Music truly is an amazing spectacle to observe, especially for those of us who reside out in the country and do not experience events of this nature on a regular basis. I wandered about watching some acts practice their craft, lost in awe at the abilities and daring displayed, when I happened to come across a particular act in the process of honing its skills.

As I stood mesmerized by the level of mastery that I saw before me, a thought came to my mind. It wasn't a good thought; it was a *great* thought!

After making some hasty arrangements, I soon was headed back to The Manor, the various individual sounds of The Festival fading into general noise the further away I got.

Now, as I had told you previously, The Duchess is a lover of music; and it just so happened that one of the acts that she absolutely *had* to hear were scheduled to perform later that day. At lunch, I casually mentioned that I too appreciated their work. I offered to accompany The Duke and Duchess down to the performance.

Later that afternoon, the three of us walked on down the path from The Manor toward The Festival. The Duchess and I were out front indicative of our enthusiasm for the act that we were about to hear while The Duke was lagging a few steps behind, when out from behind a tree stepped a man wearing a mask and flipping a very large knife in his hand!

"Not another step!" the man demanded. "Give me your valuables and no one gets hurt!"

The Duke stopped where he was, studying the man. The Duchess froze in fright; she was not used to this kind of surprise at all. Me—I stepped gallantly in front of The Duchess to shield her from any harm.

"What manner of nonsense is this?" I demanded. "Be off with you, or you shall feel my wrath!"

"The only thing that will be felt is my knife entering your flesh," the highwayman replied while displaying his honed steel with menace. "That is, if you dare to move," he added with a laugh.

I could feel The Duchess's hand tight upon my shoulder. "Don't do anything rash!" she whispered in fright. Her eyes could not leave the sight of the knife, gleaming sharp in the sunlight.

"Worry not, My Lady," I assured her in my best 'hero' voice as I moved a few steps off to the right as if to test his resolve; "I shall handle this. Yo knave," I taunted him, "what makes you so sure that your blade could even *find* my flesh?"

I was answered in a heartbeat as with a flick of his wrist, the knife was sent flying to land in the ground less than an inch from my right foot!

As in reaction to the scene enfolding before her, The Duchess immediately turned pale while becoming unsure of her feet. As she appeared ready to swoon, The Duke began to rush to her side, yet almost immediately stopped dead in his tracks.

"I said *hold*!" the highwayman commanded, his second blade appearing as if by magic in his raised throwing hand. "However, you My Lady, may feel free to faint—or collapse—or whatever it is that you ladies do," he announced with a sneer.

I glanced down at the knife that had nearly split my boot, then back up at our attacker and replied to his bravo with a simple "Missed me. Is that the best you can do?" I blustered as I kicked the knife away into the bracken.

"Oh, I can do much better than that!" he snarled as he drew back and readied his second blade to fly "Where would you like this one?" he asked in fancy politeness.

Moving further away from The Duchess so as to keep his attention on me and free up The Duke to reach his wife, I pointed to my hat. "Let's see you knock it off of my head," I mocked him; "or do you not have the stomach for such daring a maneuver?"

"Dylan, what are you *doing*?" The Duchess demanded in horror, her cuffed hand rising as if to cover her mouth. "Stop this right now before someone gets hurt!" she insisted as one who usually got her way due to the position she held in life.

I turned to speak to her face to face. Her eyes indicated the terror she was experiencing, her shaking hands covering trembling lips. "I'm not scared of this varmint," I told her much to her chagrin.

Turning back to face our assailant, I *felt* more than *saw* the flash of the knife as it flew past my eyes!

Before I could even blink, I heard the sound of metal hitting wood. Turning about ever so slowly, I saw that stuck into a tree directly behind me was my hat with his knife firmly embedded in its center!

I began to fear that The Duchess surely would faint from the encounter. I am certain that only her years of training and experience within the world of the Nobility kept her from landing flat on the grass.

"Dylan, I forbid you do anything foolish!" the Duke ordered harshly. "Stand fast!"

"You heard the man," laughed my knife-wielding foe. "I shall be gracious and not punish you for shaking in your boots, however."

"You have shown me *nothing*, Clown!" I taunted back, my voice literally dripping with disdain. I did my best to peer into his eyes, but his mask kept me from reading the mind of this man.

Off to the side I could hear The Duchess pleading with The Duke to stop me...*now*!

The Duke was just about to speak when I fired back to our assailant "Let's see just how good you *really* are," I said while taking several more steps away from my little group. "I have an object here in my pocket; at the count of three, I will fling it up into the air," I announced to the horror of my companions. "If you are worth your salt, put a blade right through its center! If you do this, you have won this day and our valuables will be yours," I offered. The casual lilt in my voice turned to iron as I assumed a stance as if ready to attack him. "But when you *fail,* as you most certainly shall, I will be upon you before you can draw more steel! The question is," I wondered as if to the air itself "are you man enough to try?"

The highwayman was taken aback by my show of bravado. Apparently he was not accustomed to receiving reactions such as mine in his line of work. "Throw away fool—it is my *fourth* blade that shall taste your blood this day!" he announced as he set himself with knife readily in hand.

The Duchess was beside herself screaming at me to stop and at the same time pleading with The Duke to make me back down!

"One," I counted.

"Dylan," The Duke said slowly and firmly, "do not tempt this man further, for he has talent with a blade!"

"So do I at the dinner table, Sir," I replied casually while quickly glancing his way. "Besides, I don't believe that this fool could even count to three," I answered bravely while facing my antagonist once again.

"Two," I announced with challenge while feeling into my pocket and putting the object I had found there into my hand. I set one foot in front of the other as if to make a charge at the man upon his throw. "Are you feeling lucky?" I asked the masked man.

The man settled himself and hefted his knife. "It's your move," was all that he said.

"Dylan...don't!" cried both The Duke and Duchess simultaneously.

It was almost as if time itself stood still waiting for the outcome of this clash, for at my yelled count of "Three!" I threw the object into the air and jumped for the man. I could hear the sound of the knife tearing through the air as it homed in on the object I had tossed.

The Duchess screamed!

The Duke dashed over to protect his wife, his strong arms grasping to keep her from collapsing onto the ground below as her knees had finally given way.

I took one step towards the mystery man, but he disappeared just as quickly as he had arrived. Where he had been standing, there was nothing...just the wind.

I turned back to face The Duke and Duchess. The Duchess was openly sobbing in his arms as he stood between her and our now-vanished assailant as if to offer himself up as a shield for the woman he loved. Neither had yet to raise their gazes from each other almost in fear of what they should discover had become of my fate.

Making certain that our knife-wielding foe had indeed gone, I then walked over to retrieve the object which I had tossed. I picked it up by the handle of the knife protruding directly from its center.

This guy really had *tremendous* ability!

Slowly covering the distance between myself and The Duke and Duchess while holding the object I had thrown in the palm of my one hand, all they could see was the hilt of the rather large knife, not the object which I had tossed. The Duke was kneeling beside his wife as she sat upon the ground fighting both the urge to faint and lose the contents of her lunch at the same time.

As I reached where they were both attempting to recover from the spectacle they had just witnessed, I worked the knife free of its bounds and tossed it away as it nothing more than a nuisance. Standing over them, their faces void of expression as if in shock, I opened my hand to let the object that I held fall to the ground in front of them for their further inspection.

They both remained as if frozen, the tear-stained visage of The Duchess having pulled away from the comfort of her husband's shoulder to view in disbelief the object that had fallen from my hand to rest before them on the warm summer grass.

Split right down the middle was the 'king' piece from a chess set!

Their stunned silence was my applause. I could read comprehension as to what had just occurred come slowly to the face of the Duke. The Duchess on the other hand was totally lost as she looked up at me, her confusion evident as all she could find herself to ask was a very stammering "Wha...what?"

I knelt down before them to see her face as I answered her directly. It was only one little *sentence*; one small group of words that each taken by themselves meant *nothing*, but when put together indicated one of the greatest moments of my life!

"*That*, My Lady... is checkmate."

I am such a dead man.

✠

It certainly is dark in the dungeon of The Manor of Arlington Green. At least I think that it is as I can't really see well enough to tell.

In reality it is not a dungeon at all; more like an old, unused wine cellar in the basement. But as it does have a lock upon it's metal lattice door, it was serving as my place of detention very nicely for the moment.

To their credit, both The Duke and The Duchess took my effort at payback very well. They both *appreciated* the intricate planning and the theatre that a trick of this magnitude required. They both *knew* down in their hearts that they had just been had by one of the best efforts they would ever see. And they both *promised* they would have some food sent to me—*eventually*—while I was being tossed into the darkness!

I was feeling very pleased with myself at that moment. I had just pulled off the *ultimate* trick— quite brilliantly, I may add. The satisfaction that I felt while watching the looks on their faces as the understanding that they had been duped dawned upon them made the odor of the poop that I had fallen into off of the roof depart from my nose for all time. I will remember those looks for the rest of my life.

However, as I gazed about into the blackness of my cell, I suddenly realized that may not be a very long time!

I did the best that I could to get comfortable as I sat on the cold stone floor, the occasional scurrying of some unknown critter in the darkness the only indication to me that my senses were still functioning—other than listening to the growling of my empty stomach that is!

Time meant nothing as I had no way of guessing the passing of minutes or hours…or days for that matter.

By and by, I could discern a lightening of the intense blackness surrounding me as a torch appeared to be descending the stairs down to my cell. I rose off of the floor to see who it was that had come to visit me.

It was Robyn, making her uncertain way down the slippery stairs with torch in one hand while her other held onto the hem of her dress. Relieved that she had reached the bottom while still on her feet, she approached my center of detention. I tried to read the expression on her face, but the flickering torch threw shadows across her delicate features.

Hanging onto the grill of my cell door, I started to chuckle and asked her if The Duke or Duchess had told her what I had pulled off?

A faint nod of her head indicated that she had been so informed as she stood before me in the darkness, the flickering of her torch my only guide to the world of sight.

"Oh, you should have seen their faces…" was all I was able to say when she stopped me dead in my tracks.

"Do you realize what you have *done?*" was all that she asked in a voice flat and without emotion. Something in her tone was causing me worry as there was no excitement at sharing in my triumph—only dare I say *sadness?*

"I pulled off a great practical joke," I replied, while trying my best to read her expression. "Is there more?" I inquired in confusion.

"And what is occurring outside of these walls right now?" she continued to query evenly. From the tightness of her grip on the torch to the arrow-straightness of her stance, I could now detect that the effort was taking all of her self-control.

"The Music Festival?" I answered hesitantly.

Something in the back of my mind told me this was not going well.

"And *where* are you?" she asked, her lips pursed as if trying her best to keep something contained within herself.

"Okay, I'm in the dungeon—pardon me, the *wine cellar,*" I answered tentatively "but I'm sure that I will be out soon; it was just a *joke* after all" I re-assured her.

Setting the torch into a stanchion on the wall, she could hold herself in no longer.

"AND WHERE DO I NEED YOU TO BE?" blasted forth from her lungs with all the force that years of vocal training and usage could produce.

I immediately understood what she meant. What an idiot I was! Amidst all of this payback nonsense, I had completely overlooked the fact that she was going to perform. The old Dylan had emerged in that I was focused only upon myself and paid no attention to anything or *anyone* else…especially her! Even if I was let out tomorrow, that would be too late as she needed me *now* to help get her through what was to her a terrifying fear—and I couldn't be there! Never before had I felt like such a fool, and that truly is saying a lot.

"Don't worry," I told her hopefully, "I will think of something to get out of here."

"That's what got you *here* in the first place!" she cried, her pent-up emotion finally getting the best of her. "When are you going to *grow up* Dylan?" she demanded or *begged* as I couldn't discern which. "When is it going to be enough for you?"

I couldn't even answer her, for there was nothing that I could say.

She was totally right.

"Where are the Duke and Duchess now?" I asked her, hanging my head in shame. I could not find the strength within myself to look into her eyes and read what I knew to be there.

"They are at The Festival enjoying the sounds of beautiful music," she responded, wiping her eyes on the edge of her dress. "That is where *we* should be, not stuck down here in this prison."

"Can you get a message to them for me?" I asked while staring at the floor. I still could not look her in the eye, for I did not want to see the despair that I could hear so readily in her voice. "Can you ask them to come here as soon as it is convenient?" I quietly asked.

"For what purpose?" she inquired, her anger now taking over from her pain. "So that you can try to *trip* them as they come down the stairs perhaps? Maybe you can attempt to catch a rat and fling it down The Duchess's bodice?" she asked as she paced nervously about. "No, I think that you have finally found your rightful place," she told me, her head drooping as her pain won out once again; "down here among the rats and the vermin."

There was nothing that I could say to give her any sense of comfort. I was being crushed by the woman I loved. At that moment I realized that maybe she was right and that I *should* remain here until I perished. It was my turn now to pace within my confines as I did my best to rally what little self-esteem that I had left.

"I need to get out of here so we can get you ready for tomorrow," I tried hopefully once I could find my voice.

She shook her head sadly, tears welling in her eyes. "There is *nothing* to prepare," she said barely above a whisper; "I am withdrawing from the competition."

No…no…no; what have I done? I took all of her confidence that had been built up from the children's performance this morning and dashed it to pieces by my own selfishness! The wrenching of her soul that I had caused may be irreparable.

"Don't *say* that!" I pleaded. "You *must* perform. You have much too much talent and ability to just throw away your opportunity. You *must* reconsider!" I begged, throwing my arms through the grate of the doorway in an effort to hold her. "I want to see you out-perform all of those others; that would make me so proud of you."

"Proud!" she cried while backing away from my attempted touch. "You want to be proud of *me*? For what purpose? What good is it for you to be proud of me due to an effort that lasts but a few *moments* when I spend every waking day waiting to be able to say the same of you?"

She resumed her pacing outside the cell door. I could tell that this was really hurting her. There was *nothing* for me to say; once again I hung my head in shame. I could not look within her eyes as she continued to tear me too pieces. Listening to the pain in her voice, I'm not so sure that I was the one that was hurting the most by what she was telling me there in the flickering darkness.

"You profess this great *love* for me," she continued as if measuring her words carefully, "yet where will that lead us, Dylan? Will you still be throwing snowballs at me five years from now? Am I to stand by and watch my True-Love be thrown in the cells *again* because his precious ego made him win a hearty game of one-upmanship?" she asked, tearing at my heart. "Or maybe…just maybe you think that it would *impress* me if any of those throws had been off in the slightest and I could be kneeling by you on your *deathbed*?" she inquired in a way that I knew had no answer.

"*Where* does it lead, Dylan, this great professed love of yours—of ours? Where does it lead?"

Silence hung in the air heavier than the darkness being chased by the flickering of her torch flame. I tried to come up with an answer that was the truth, for was all that she would believe now—if even that!

"Robyn," I began while finally lifting my eyes to hers, "I know that in many ways I still act the child. I would *like* to tell you that it is something that I will outgrow, but I don't believe that," I admitted; "and *neither* do you. It is a large part of me that wants to want to laugh and enjoy special moments; unfortunately, I get lost so easily that I forget that the precious moments that I want to spend are truly with *you*."

I began my pacing once again as I searched within my soul for the words that could reach her. For a Teller-of-Tales, telling the truth can be a *very* difficult thing!

"I truly *do* love you as I have no other—or ever will," I continued as I returned to the gateway. "I believe you *know* that to be true just as I know that your love for *me* is real."

This really was beginning to hurt, for I had never been this honest before—especially with myself.

The light from her flickering torch played upon her face in a way that reminded me of the love seat and the fire during the Holiday.

How stupid could I have been? I gazed into her eyes brimming with tears. I felt like I could rip myself apart for the damage and hurt that I had done to her.

"It would be *easy* for me to promise to you here and now that I will become a different man," I told her from my heart. "In many ways, I *do* know this to be true. But I also know that I will still be Dylan, for he I am and he I will remain. I will never *be* that Brave Knight riding a white horse to sweep you away to everlasting happiness in some far-off Manor," I said, as tears began to well in my own eyes; "and I *do* wish that it were so. You have *no idea* how I wish that it were so! For then you would be proud of me when you look up to me, and I could see how this great love that you have for me *could* be real."

My voice broke with emotion as I continued. "I would then be someone that would have *earned* what you have freely given me and not some fool that is only capable of producing stories and tales of the hearty deeds of others."

I don't believe that I was saying these words, but as I was finally being truthful, I didn't know where to stop.

"That is why you need to be in the competition and do your best," I told her in shaky voice. "You have more than enough talent and ability to win this effort; we both know that to be truth. And by winning, you would have the opportunity to be free; free to go where you can be successful and make your name. And" I continued through the pain in my heart "free of *me*."

She looked long and hard into my eyes.

"Is *that* what you think I *want*?" she finally asked, her eyes glistening in the torchlight.

"No, My Love," I answered quietly; "that is what I think that you *need*."

I turned and walked to the farthest corner of the cell, where the darkness hid my tears. For I had given to her the one motivation to succeed that I could under the circumstances, and the pain of it reached down to my very heart!

She lingered a few moments, but we both knew that this conversation was ended. Silently she removed the torch from the stanchion and proceeded to slowly climb the stairs. Pausing before she made it halfway up, Robyn turned to face me once again. "It appears that I am destined to lose you at any Festival of Music that I enter," I was told as if the irony of the situation was more than could be believed. And then she was gone, as the light of my life began to flicker and die—and once again I was truly left behind in the dark.

I woke somewhat later—I did not know the time as hours do not gather in the darkness—only to realize that my head was badly hurting. Reaching hand to forehead, I felt the unmistakable texture of caked dried blood. Then I remembered...I had actually been *smashing* my head against the hard stone of my prison as if to free myself of my pain in the only way I could at the moment; endless sleep! But the blissful ignorance of sleep comes to an end, returning one to the land of despair fresh and free to hurt once again.

I learned a valuable lesson that day; a man can run from everything and everyone but *himself*, for he cannot outrun the pain in his heart.

Were that it be so!

I do not know how long I remained in the darkness, but whether it was weakness from lack of food and drink or weariness of the soul, I mercifully fell back into a fitful sleep.

When I awoke once again, light had returned into my world. My squinting eyes could see that I had a visitor; it was The Duke himself.

He was sitting at a small table that had magically appeared at the bottom of the stairs, eating a meal and drinking wine. I quickly realized how hungry and thirsty I was—I am sure that was his intent. He just sat looking at me, his gaze bore into me as if it were the sharpest lance.

This was one time when I knew to keep my mouth shut!

Okay, we all know that is impossible for me, but I did honestly *try*.

"Sir," I began, "I want to apologize ..." was as far as I got. At his command of "Be quiet!" for once I *did* as I was told.

I was trying to read his expression as he was mine. By the blank stares on both of our faces, only a long conversation would solve this conundrum.

"I hope that you are *proud* of yourself," he said, reaching for some steaming hot bread.

"Sir, I was at first," I told him, tearing my eyes off the bread and back to his face, "for I thought that I had pulled off something special. But I do wish you to know that I feel that way no more."

"Why is that?" he inquired between bites.

"I was not paying attention to the *price* of the act—only the result," I admitted. "I wanted to win what I saw was a competition; now I realize that in 'winning', I have *lost* so much that I held dear. The consequences of what I have done will ring true through my life for the rest of my days," I said sadly, withdrawing deeper into my pain. "Whether I spend them in here with the rats or somewhere in the light of the sun makes little difference."

He continued to peer at me through the bars of my prison almost as if he was judging my responses to determine my fate. Apparently I was going to get another heaping helping of the truth.

"And what is it that you have lost?" he inquired while taking a sip of wine.

I hung my head. "I have lost the respect that you and The Duchess have so freely given me, I have lost the love of my Beautiful Lady, I have thrown away my personal integrity—shall I continue, or is that enough for now?" I asked sadly.

"I would say that is enough—for now. So tell me, how do you think that Robyn *did* for her performance...*alone?*"

He really was going right for the throat! Under the circumstances I would have done the same.

"I pray that she was able to finally realize that she had the talent and ability to win the event with confidence," I answered him eventually once the depth of his question allowed me to speak, "but I know that would not be the case. She would pay more attention in her mind to me and my stupidity than to her own performance. I cannot imagine *how* she did," I told him with regret in my voice. "I do hope that she has won for her own benefit."

"And what benefit would that be?" he inquired with curiosity. I guess I was only to get one sentence questions from him for a while.

"So that she can gain confidence in her abilities and go create a life for herself that will bring her satisfaction, fame, and especially *happiness*," I told him. "In short, a life that would be free from *me*."

He continued studying me. His expression had not changed, nor the tone of his inquiries. "Is that what you think that she wants?" he asked eventually.

Again with the one sentence.

"It is what I think that she *needs*...and what she deserves," I answered, the inescapable tone of unhappiness obvious in my response. "She should have all the respect that her talent can bring—but most importantly, she should have someone who can be worthy of the *love* that she brings." I looked directly into his eyes when I admitted "She deserves better than me...we both *know* that to be true."

His head cocked back as if he had just been greatly surprised. "Do we now?" he asked in response. "And just how have we both come to that realization?" he wondered openly.

At least we were up *two* sentences now; progress was being made.

"She could claim *any* man in the Realm," I told him. "She is young, beautiful, sweet, talented, and the most wonderful of women." I smiled as I pictured her while describing her attributes. "Why should she *settle* for me?" I asked him directly. "Should she settle for *me* just because I am here and so is she?"

My query was met by complete silence that seemed to hover within the very air.

"You know; I believe that you may be right," was his eventual response.

I must admit that was not what I was hoping to hear from him. Maybe a nice '*You're wrong Dylan, you are right for her*' or something similar would have been welcome—*anything* to hang a little hope onto.

He paused for just a moment before he began his explanation. "I believe that she *could* have almost any man in the Realm, and exactly for the reasons that you have just mentioned," he said pointing to me. "The trouble is; it is *you* that she wants."

I did have to agree with him there. "Wants yes…but *deserves*? What do I bring to the table that she could *possibly* want?" I asked in confusion.

This had become a very interesting conversation. I am certain that the Duke had come down here to cut me to pieces, and here he was going to be listing some of my positive aspects.

If there were any to be found.

Sometimes I think that I just don't understand life at all!

"Are you really that blind from only a short time in the darkness?" he asked amazed. "Robyn does not see you with the eyes of *reality*, she sees you from the eyes of *love*," he explained. "The eyes of reality come later when the newness of your relationship wears off. She will have *plenty* of time then to list your many failings," he chuckled deeply. "To her, you and you *alone* are the man for her. And that is, and I don't believe that I am saying this, because of all of the positive qualities that you possess—in addition to the others *too,* of course. She is in love with *Dylan,*" he told me evenly, "not some Dylan that does not exist."

I thought quietly about that one for a moment.

"And don't sell yourself so short, My Friend," he continued. "For you are intelligent and *very* clever as we have recently discovered," he said with the beginnings of a grin. "You are both loyal and capable as under your direction the school has been highly successful, you dealt with this 'Trysto' most brilliantly, and you have this *uncanny* knack of accomplishing any task that you are given once you set your mind to it. All in all," he smiled, "that is a pretty good start don't you think?"

I found myself chuckling at the unreality of this discussion.

The Duke immediately asked me what was so funny, his slight grin vanishing as if a puff of smoke.

"It is the irony of the situation, Sir," I replied. "Here you are boasting of my talents, when I figured that you would be berating me for the stupidity of my acts! It does seem slightly warped, does it not?" I asked truthfully.

"Never *expect* anything out of life," he answered in a fatherly tone," or you will close yourself off to the opportunity of enjoying its amazement. Besides," he said as he handed me a glass of wine, "I know you rather well. I figured that you would be busy tearing yourself up over this matter better than I *ever* could." He pointed to my forehead. "From the looks of your head, I believe that I was quite right!"

I gladly accepted the wine and drank freely.

Feeling its instant refreshing effect, I gather up all of my emotional reserves. "You have not yet said," I asked, dreading his response; "how *did* Robyn do?"

"No idea," he answered, "for she has not yet performed. She goes on stage in about an hour from now."

Did I hear him right? She had not *yet* done her song. Then I still had time to make things right!

"I don't suppose that your visit would be timed due to her schedule?" I inquired, taking another sip of wine.

"I think that we both know the answer to that one," he replied. "Robyn deserves the opportunity to be her best—you were absolutely *right* about that. For some odd reason, the girl seems to think that it is *you* that brings out the best in her. Poor misguided Lass," he said shaking his head.

"I'm not so sure that she still has the same opinion of me," I told him. "After the tongue lashing I got from her earlier, I may be the *last* person on this earth that she may want to see right now."

"*Want* to see? Quite possibly," he agreed. "*Need* to see; now that is a different story. You have become her stability and a source of her strength," he went on. "Right now she is waffling between her fear and nervousness of being on the stage to her anger at you for not being there."

I had to agree with him. "I know this to be true," I admitted.

We both knew where this was going; I might as well get it there as quickly as possible. "So," I inquired matter-of-factly, "do you know of any way that we can rectify this situation?"

He looked long and hard at me. "Don't be so damn smug, or I will *leave* you in there!" he scolded me. "I am offering you a parole—nothing more. You will be released until she does her performance, then it is right back inside. That is my offer; take it or leave it."

"There are no words to properly thank you, Sir," I said. "Not so much for myself, but for Robyn's sake. I don't think that I could have lived with myself if I couldn't be there now when she needs me the most."

"That is as I thought," he said, taking a set of keys from his tunic and unlocking the door. "I do suggest that you be on your best behavior however."

"No problem there, Sir," I assured him. "I will not do anything to embarrass you."

"Oh, it's not *me*," he replied offhandedly. "It's *The Duchess* you need be worried about! I'm not putting you back in your cell for further punishment," he said as we began to ascend the stairs; "it is for your own *protection*! If I left you out for good, you may never have the opportunity to have children."

"A bit miffed at me still, is she?" I inquired.

"Oh, you have *no* idea!" he replied. "In fact, you had better stay behind the stage during Robyn's performance—unless you wish to accompany her in a very high voice!"

"And Dylan…"

"Yes Sir."

"If you *ever* repeat what I am about to tell you to *anyone*, I *will* have you locked in the kitchen with my wife and all of those sharp knives—do you understand?"

"Perfectly Sir," I assured him.

"That really was a very good ploy you just pulled off," he chuckled while patting me on the back.

"Thank you Sir…never heard it."

"Never said it."

Festive Departure?

Cleaning the remaining dried blood off of my forehead, I quickly dressed and headed down towards The Festival. There is *no way* that I was going to miss Robyn's performance after the break that I had received.

There is also *no way* that I was going to ever admit what the Duke had said to me down there in the cellar.

And as there is definitely *no way* that I am going to be spotted by The Duchess until she cools off, which is why I was sneaking down to The Festival tree by tree. I am sure that I looked absolutely ridiculous.

Oh, like *that's* something different!

By my reckoning, I had about 30 minutes until Robyn would be on stage; I kept going forward for I knew what I had to do. More importantly, I finally knew what I *wanted* to do.

Tree by tree, bush by bush, I made my way closer and closer to The Festival grounds.

The sounds of excellent music and singing, along with the barkers calling out their wares grew stronger and stronger as did those amazing aromas. Pennants of all the colors in the rainbow fluttered in the gentle breeze. I quickly slipped into the crowd, which was fortunately flowing toward the main stage—and towards my Robyn.

Apparently, I had misjudged the popularity of this event, for there were not hundreds of people in attendance—there were *thousands*! This would truly be a Festival of Music that would be remembered for years to come.

I broke from the crowd and made my way to the rear of the stage. Fortunately, the attendants remembered me from yesterday's choir performance, for I was allowed to enter the backstage area without question. Inquiring as to where Robyn could be found, I was directed towards a red curtain off to the left.

That simple red curtain stared me right in the face; all I had to do was move it aside, and I would get my chance to talk to Robyn.

Just had to *move* that old red curtain there.

Yep, that's all it would take—just moving aside that red curtain hanging *right* there!

I must admit that I was truly scared, but I was proud of myself in that I was more adamant. I reached for the curtain and pushed it aside.

There was my beautiful Robyn, along with—oh My God!

The Duchess!

I immediately looked around for any sharp objects that could be thrown in my direction. From the look that I was getting from her, she would have gladly fired off anything she could find with no regret.

I spoke quickly before she had the chance for any verbal attacks. "My Lady," I began, "I will ask for your forgiveness at the first opportunity there is—*after* I speak with Robyn. You may even have your revenge in any way that you see fit," I offered while trying not to imagine what she would wish to do, "but for now, and I don't believe that I am talking this way, I must ask you to *leave*."

For a moment we just stood there staring at each other, with neither willing to speak first.

I could not decide what her expression was at that moment. The surprise of me showing up must have worn off by then. Perhaps she was contemplating calling the guards? Or was it the realization that she would have me just where she wanted me in the very near future? Or maybe—just *maybe*—I caught a small gleam of respect and appreciation in that I was there at all.

In any event, she reached over to give Robyn a hug, whispered in her ear, and slowly walked past me to the curtain. "Remember Dear, that when you win, you will be free of this *oaf* forever," she called back, obviously for my benefit.

I really hope what was *not* obvious was the fact that I was purposely positioning myself so that I would not have my open back towards The Duchess—until with a swish of the curtain, she was gone. It would be quite a while before I could feel comfortable doing *that* again!

I gazed over to where Robyn was standing. She was doing her best to ignore the fact that I was even there by holding her head down and not looking into my face. I guess that she would not have to *see* me after all, but she did have to *listen* to me. Whether I had to fight off all of The Festival guards to get it done, she was going to hear what I had to say!

During my time in the dungeon, I had tried to prepare what I was going to say to begin this conversation if I ever got the chance. But facing her now, I realized that any prepared notion would not do. Having messed up as badly as I had, it was from the heart that I would have to speak to reach her.

"So… ah, the music sounds pretty good out there," I observed while moving a little closer.

So much for speaking from the *heart*; I guess I just had to be me.

My words were met with silence as she continued to stare at the floor as if I wasn't there.

"So…who is that out there now?" I asked, hoping once again to get some kind of reply.

This time I got a muffled mumble for an answer. I took that to be a positive response as she had done *something*, so I plowed on ahead.

"*Who* was that?" I inquired again while moving a bit closer to her.

"Fifty Pence!" she replied sharply with her hands placed defiantly on her hips.

While her response was anything but cordial, inwardly I breathed a sigh of relief as her eyes had finally turned away from the floor and were staring at a spot directly over my head. I don't know, maybe she was imagining a large rock about to fall on my head there, but at least I was drawing her out.

"Oh please, don't screw this up!" I thought to myself. While I was far from confident, I *was* finding strength to continue from what I believed to be a successful beginning.

"Yeah, I heard that he was pretty good," I said, keeping my voice low key. "Sounds like you just might have some competition there."

"Whatever," was all I got in return.

Darn, I was going backwards rapidly! It was time to take the chance of my life and break out from these one-word answers one way or another.

"You know, I heard a lot of people talking outside before I came in," I told her with a casual air that in no way reflected the turmoil churning within me. "They all agreed that you possibly *could* have won if he hadn't shown up—that and if you weren't a *girl* of course."

I knew from experience that this subject was one that angered her no end, and I prayed that I would get *some* reaction out of her by making such a statement.

Oh, I got a *reaction* all right!

She turned to face me now with fire in her eyes! "*Who* said that I couldn't win just because I was a woman?" she demanded.

"Oh, just people walking around outside…nobody special," I offered while pointing to the outside. "The word around The Festival is that the odds makers are giving 5 to 1 that he will win. That's pretty good, isn't it?" I asked. "I don't have any money, but if you would loan me some of yours, I could go place a bet on you," I offered while shrugging my shoulders for effect. "Who knows, *maybe* you could possibly win after all."

If I thought that she might have been angry before, she was downright *livid* now! Her chest rose and dove rapidly as she strove to calm herself—which if I may say so was not necessarily a terrible thing to observe.

Another thing that I had observed was that she was wearing the green dress that I had bought her, along with the necklace that held the small red stone she had gotten from me. Her hair was in a long double braid, which must have been *strictly* co-incidence as that is how I like it the best.

I said nothing about any of this—at least not *yet*; it was not the time for it yet.

"I guess not," I said casually "as I'm into The Duke for *enough* money as it is."

That one did it! She got right into my face, her rapid breath escaping through clenched teeth to flow down my chest. As she had still not said anything, even more *drastic* measures were being called for.

Reaching down and taking firm hold of her right hand, I held it tight… and slapped myself directly across the face with it!

Part of her anger subsided to be replaced by surprise and confusion. Not *enough*, but it was a start. I kept hold of her hand and slapped myself with it once again! These were not little love taps either, as I could feel my face turning red. Fortunately, I could also feel her tension and anger begin to lessen by the loosening of her hand.

Standing there while waiting for my prayers to be answered within the depths of Robyn's reactions, the sounds of The Festival outside seemed to dim and fade in my ears as if the two of us were the only ones within a mile of that stage.

Her gently shaking head fell to stare at the floor once again. I could see in her eyes that she was very confused.

I reached down to gently raise her head until her eyes met mine. I quietly asked her "Do you want to do that by yourself without my help?"

Wham! She clobbered me right across the chops!

That one was harder than any that I had helped her with. I guarantee that The Duchess would have been *really* proud of what she had just done.

Her hands fell to her sides as she began quietly to weep. "I hate you," was all that she could say.

I reached out to hold her tightly; she did not fight to get away. Her slight body continued to shudder as she sobbed, small trickles of tears running down my neck. "I know that you do," I whispered into her ear while she remained nestled in my arms. I gently kissed her check as I once more agreed "I know that you do."

"You are the most obnoxious, childish, self-centered clod that I have ever laid eyes on," she said in between sobs, "and I hate you." There was no anger in her voice now; more *remorse* I would gauge it to be.

"You forgot simple-minded, weasel-faced, and idiotic," I offered, chuckling just a touch.

To my great relief, the shuddering sobbing began to ebb as eventually she giggled a bit too.

She finally raised her eyes to mine. "And stupid, mangy, *and* selfish," she added while exhibiting the beginning of a smile; "don't forget those."

"What do you mean *mangy?*" I demanded as if I was greatly surprised. "I'm not mangy."

"Yes you are," she said as she ran her fingers through my hair. "At least you are until you get this hair trimmed."

Crisis overcome!

We still had about ten minutes before she was scheduled to perform. I led her over to sit in a chair while proceeding to kneel down before her.

Holding her hands, eyes locked on each others, I was getting the chance to say what I had so desperately wanted to while still within the darkness of my cell.

"Robyn…My Love," I began as I gazed into her big beautiful eyes, "I know that I do some incredibly *stupid* things. I will be the first to agree with that statement—and probably not the last," I freely admitted.

Amidst the remnants of tears, a small laugh escaped from her.

"But you must believe me that I would not *intentionally* do anything to hurt you," I said in all seriousness. "I try hard not to; yet in spite of that, I know that I do."

She nodded her head slightly, agreeing with me as she wiped her eyes dry.

"I know that I don't *deserve* you," I told her honestly.

Larger head nod, but this time accompanied with a beautiful smile.

"I just want you to be happy," I told her sincerely. "I really think that I keep you from feeling that way."

She started to shake her head no, but I stopped her.

"Yes I do—I *know* that I do. I just want you to know that I am so *proud*…so *very* proud of you for remaining in this competition," I said while matching the width of her smile with one of my own. "I knew that you had that kind of inner strength, even if you didn't."

"It is *you* that gives me strength," she whispered.

"Me? How do I give you strength?" I asked with a tilt of my head as her answer honestly surprised me.

"By believing in me as much as you do," she answered. "When I see myself through your eyes, I realize how much you *do* believe in me; I take strength from that knowledge," I was told. "For if you have someone who thinks so much of you, you *have* to be worthy of that faith," she said with certainty.

"Oh you are so worthy…you most certainly are!" I told her readily. "And I want you to know that my opinion has nothing to do with the love that I hold for you."

She appeared to be confused by that statement, so I explained myself further. For one very beautiful moment, one would think that the sun shone through my eyes as I spoke what I knew to be true.

"If I were blind, deaf, and dumb, I would still know when you walked into the room," I told her tenderly. "I would *feel* your sweet voice as you began in song, for even the blind know when the sun shines fully on their faces! Even the deaf could *see* the pure joy in your eyes and in your heart as you sang! Even the dumb would clap and rejoice with the treasure that you have given them."

"You speak of faith?" I asked her. "I have much more than just *faith* in you," I said, nodding my head most positively. "I *know* the many qualities that you have; your musical talents are only one of the many." My voice trailed off into a mere whisper as I repeated very adamantly "I *know*!"

Her eyes began to fill with tears.

Is that all I make this girl do?

"That is why I want so badly for you to win this competition," I told her while rising to my feet. Looking down onto the face of an angel, I told her words that I did not want to reveal yet could not in good conscious withhold for my own personal gain. "I could be selfish and try to keep you all to myself, but that would not be fair to you. You deserve to perform before Royalty, for that is how you make *me* feel when I hear you…as if I were a King! How can I keep that all to myself?" I asked honestly.

"All you have to do is ask," she said quietly.

I so wanted to take her in my arms and never let go.

"A bird needs to fly," was all that I could say to her.

"And a bird without a nest can't survive," she answered back with those big doe eyes of hers boring directly into my soul.

"There are only a few minutes left before you go out there," I reminded her as I got to my feet to go. "You need to concentrate on the task at hand, so I will leave you now."

She shook her head in disbelief. "How can you *say* this?" she asked, the fire in her eyes returning once again! "You say that I need to concentrate and perform when you are taking *away* any concentration that I may have? You are pulling away my rock when I need its foundation the most!" she cried incredulously.

She rose from her seat to face me directly. "Did you come out of the darkness of your cell only to assure my *inability* to perform?" she asked in confusion and rising anger. "Why would you do that if you say that you would never hurt me, Dylan? Just what *did* you come here for?" she demanded!

I got back down on one knee before her. Taking her hands once again into mine, I was able to finally tell her what I so desperately had wanted to for so long. "To ask you to marry me," was all that I said.

If the look of confusion on her face was any indication, her head must have been reeling. "*What* did you just ask?" she said quietly, as if afraid to breathe.

"I am asking you to be my wife," I told her with a smile. "I know that I have no right to ask this of you after how I have treated you, and I do realize that no matter how hard I try I will continue to do boneheaded stunts, and I probably will still try to hit you with a snowball even when we are old and feeble; but you will have all that I am—the good *with* the bad. That is, if you will *have* me," I said, my general lack of confidence growing stronger as the depth of what I had just said registered into my head as it flowed from my heart.

She sat still as if incapable of moving, her eyes closed as if asleep.

It was at that exact moment that a stagehand stuck his head into the curtain and announced that it was time…she was on.

I stood and took her over to put her lyre into her hands. As if sleepwalking, she offered no resistance. Holding her tightly, I whispered "Go and make me even prouder."

Slowly she walked to her entry point for the stage. She turned to face me, offering cryptically "You will have your answer," and then she was gone.

A *huge* greeting of applause and cheering met her as she walked out onto the platform. I didn't care a lick about the retaliation from The Duchess as I made my way out to the very *front* of the stage. I was going to see her perform; but more importantly I was assuring her that I was there for her...now and *forever* if she would have me.

The noise slowly quieted as she sat upon a wooden stool in the middle of the stage. Her hands appeared to me to be steady as she set her lyre at the ready. I made certain that she could *see* me as she scanned the crowd, for I had told her that I would always be there. I just hoped that seeing such a multitude before her would not give her pause to fear. She saw me standing among the many and gave me a smile as if she had eyes only for me.

I tried to figure what she was thinking from the way she was sitting, from the tilt of her head, or anything that could give me an idea of what her answer would be. The more that I wondered at what she would say the more scared that I became!

What if she said *no*?

"Thank you so much for that wonderful greeting," she announced, some slight hesitation in her voice. Fortunately, it became stronger and filled with more confidence as she went on to address the crowd loudly enough for all to hear. "There certainly are some *excellent* performers here this day, aren't there?" she asked.

They howled and clapped some more. Eventually they were quiet once again.

"I want to play a special song for you here today," she told her anxious audience.

I suddenly realized that I had never heard the melody that she had joined with my words; if after what I had done they were going to still be the words that I had written for her, I had no clue.

"It was written for me by a very special friend of mine," she said while adjusting her lyre in her lap.

So I was just a *friend*? Was *that* her answer to my big question?

"This song is a beautiful ballad," she continued, "but I have decided to make some changes to it here for you today."

Changes!

She was making changes to my song?

My mind went back into defense mode as I thought *'Fine—if that's the way it's going to be'*!

"You see," she explained further, "originally this beautiful song was titled 'Robyn' by its author. But now...now I have titled this work 'Dylan'. I hope that you enjoy it as much as *I* do in singing it here for you today."

What was it called?

Did I hear that right?

Did she just say my *name*?

The crowd came to a complete silence. The reputation of her talent proceeded her, and they were anticipating an enjoyable and quite memorable performance.

With a haunting smile etched upon her face, she stroked the strings of her lyre with precision; the lifting tones seemed to float out onto the breeze. A chill came over me as she began to sing.

Not a sound could be heard from the hundreds if not thousands of people poised there before her. As if quarried from the very rock of the earth, they sat there motionless—some with mouths open, others with smiles of contentment on their faces.

"Go Baby...*go*!" I soundlessly encouraged her.

If the sound of the lyre was silver, then her voice was pure gold!

I could never find the words to describe the beauty that these fortunate people were treated to that afternoon. I know that I am supposed to be able to do that; it's my job. But...well that's all I will say about that.

Throughout her entire performance, the audience sat as if stunned!

Reaching the last note of her song, she set down her lyre and rose to face them only to be greeted by a hushed silence. Then as if one, the entire crowd rose to their feet and *erupted* in an applause that seemed to last forever!

A very happy and I believe more than slightly *relieved* Robyn smiled widely as she took first one bow...and then another...and yet another. The audience would not stop their applause. Every person there wanted to be part of the show of appreciation for what they had just enjoyed.

They *needed* to be.

And the song? The one that used to be called 'Robyn', but forever more would be known as 'Dylan'?

It goes like this:

DYLAN

There was a time not long ago
When all that I had was me
And the world seemed a place large, empty and cold.
I had smiles I could not share,
My dreams...no one would care,
I had a story of my life that never was told.

All of my memories I could not join
With someone who had ever been there,
The smiles on my face were not attached to my heart.
With no arms to hide in,
No one to confide in,

One day would end, then another would start

The first time I met you,
You were just another
Of the people and faces I'd seen.
Yet day after day,
The more that I saw you,
We made memories…and I hoped for my dreams.

What, oh what am I to you?
Do you feel in your heart as I do?
I am ready to give you the me that I am.
And I pray I will get that from you.

And then as in shock,
One day I did listen,
And I knew that in you I would trust.
You talked not of you,
You mentioned not me,
But the word that I heard then was us.

How can you describe
The sound that is sunshine?
Or explain you an ocean or sea?
To someone who never
Has seen either one;
Thus this feeling of love was to me.

I'm only beginning
To search in the depths

Of the happiness that you do provide.
Already I need you,
I never will leave you;
And I see all the same in your eyes.

Yes, there once was a time,
When the world was so empty
It could fit in the palm of my hand.
And now I am filled
With a love that is growing;
I'm becoming the me that I can.

Personally, I think that my fiance did a pretty good job!

City Snickers

I believe I may be the most hated man within the Realm!

No, it's not The Duchess *this* time, although I do get the impression that all is not forgiven there yet. But as I am now betrothed to Robyn, she cannot very well use those knives in the way The Duke had insinuated, so I am not *quite* so worried.

No, the reason for my infamy is of course the fact how due to my asking Robyn to be my wife, she has decided she will not be giving performances throughout the Realm as the winner of the Festival of Music. I told her how she should go, and that I would visit as I could, but she would not listen. She says she has a much larger more *important* job to do here; apparently she has some strange notion I need looking after.

Where could she have possibly gotten *that* idea?

But it is the second argument she makes which I cannot deny—after the performance she gave at The Festival, how could she ever surpass that again? She makes a very good point, for how can one improve on perfection? Which of course leads me to wonder how I can possibly improve *myself*, which is quite another matter altogether.

While this has become a loss for the lovers of music throughout, it undoubtedly has increased the reputation of The Manor. Robyn always entertains for the guests of The Duke and Duchess at their many dinner parties, and there has not been a single rejection of an offered invitation since that day. She is constantly being bombarded with requests to perform the famous song 'Dylan', yet she politely refuses each request. She will gladly sing any other song which is requested; however, she insists she will only replicate this tune one more time on a very special day.

I don't know, maybe it's for her birthday or something.

Once The Festival was over, all of the carts carrying the brightly colored tents as well as subdued entrants slowly limped their way out onto the dusty roads leading away from Arlington Green. Mounds of garbage and trash went up in smoke as caretakers did their best to clean the fields of any evidence of the event.

With the ending of The Festival, we began to get back to normal around The Manor ...if such is even *possible* for us. We teachers got back into the rhythm of the classroom as school returned in full session, formerly wide-eyed children having to once again focus upon their studies.

And most importantly, I needed to find a new fishing spot.

So *much* to do.

It was at dinner one evening after things had finally quieted down when The Duke informed us how our Staff would be increasing by one as a new member would be joining us shortly—but who this person was or for what their duties would be he would not tell us.

Okay, so now I need to add another item to the list as I have to find out about this new person too; you know how nosy I am.

I had the opportunity to do just that, when Bryce and I were summoned by The Duke and asked to ride to the city in order to pick up a new carriage which he had ordered for The Duchess. For some reason, Sir Preston would be accompanying the two of us— probably to keep us out of trouble I suppose. We also were asked to pick up any correspondence for The Manor waiting there, especially any from an individual named Constance.

As we mounted our horses to begin our journey, all my curious mind had to work with was that a female named Constance (age unknown) was coming to The Manor whose job function could be anything with the exception of a Teller-of-Tales or a Singer. I figure this as Robyn has proven herself to be a talent without peer, and I owe The Duke so much money that he *has* to keep me around.

We made good time upon the road, and soon we were in the heart of the city. After acquiring what to me appeared to be correspondence which gave me no clue, we slowly rode down the cobblestone streets towards the stables where the carriage was to be found, when I could not help noticing a scuffle going on in one of the side streets just as we were passing.

Reigning in my horse, I stopped to see what the trouble was.

A small fight had erupted among a group of boys for who knows what reason. I was able to identify two of the combatants as being older boys from our village. I did not like the way they were being ridiculed and shoved around by some of what had to be city kids. Words like "Go back to your hog farm" and "It's nice to see that you can wear your Grandfather's clothes" were being bandied about. Apparently these city kids thought that due to their opportunity to have nice clothing and such, they were much better than our own village children.

The boys in question were two brothers—Miles and Terrance *Farmer*, which I am certain did not help the situation. They stood back-to-back, facing down five city kids looking for a fight.

Now, call me nosy if you want, but at five against two, I did not care for those odds at all. I turned my horse about and proceeded slowly down the lane until I was almost on top of the group.

"So what's this all about then?" I inquired as I casually reigned in my mount and stopped to hear their story.

"What this *is about* is none of your business!" said the older and larger of the City Boys. "Or are you a Hog Farmer too?" he asked with disdain as he looked me over. I was not dressed as a man of the city—darned proud of it too if the truth be known.

"No, can't say that I am," I answered him evenly as I was keeping my tone mellow in spite of the fact that my blood was beginning to boil!

"Then you may as well turn that horse around and be about your business," was his smart retort. Apparently the other four boys must have thought him to be incredibly funny as they laughed, succeeding in puffing up the confidence and courage of the bigger one.

By this time, Bryce and Sir Preston had doubled back looking for me. When they saw what was happening they split up; Bryce to block the far entrance to the alley while Sir Preston came up behind me.

"I *am* being about my business," I answered the little so-and-so. "I am about the business of evening up some odds. Five on five seems somehow fairer to me; does it not to you?" I queried happily.

They scanned the situation; five bullies against two smaller kids were acceptable. But five on five, when three of the five are carrying weapons is quite another matter!

The City Kids opened the circle which they had formed around the Farmer Boys to let them go. I maneuvered my mount in between the two groups and motioned for the Farmers to come over by my horse.

"You boys tolerable?" I asked while quickly checking them over. There was a bit of a bloody nose and a fat lip evident, but apparently no major damage had been done other than some torn clothes and bruised attitudes. "So what is this all about?" I asked of the Farmer Boys.

Miles, the older of the two answered me. "We are here on an errand for our father who is ill," he began. "We were done and just leaving the city when these boys jumped us. It seems that they believe themselves to be superior to us farm boys," he said wiping fresh blood from his nose onto his sleeve while his eyes flashed in anger at the notion.

The bigger of the City Kids reacted poorly to that statement. "Darn right we are better than you!" he announced while looking down his nose at the Farmers. "You have the nerve to come into our city with *those* clothes and dirt on your faces?" he asked condescendingly. "We would have showed them just how much better we are than them if *you* hadn't come along and saved them," he sneered in my direction as he lunged forward in an effort to renew the battle once again.

Positioning my mount to act as a shield, I protected the Farmers while steadily backing the city boys into a corner from which they could not escape.

"Oh, I'm not here to save them from *you*," I responded casually; "I am here to save you from *them*!"

My statement brought a hearty laugh from all of the City Kids. Several of them began to pull knives from sheaths hidden about their persons. The sound of Sir Preston's sword clearing its scabbard stopped them dead in their tracks; the knives disappeared just as quickly as they had appeared. Yet there must have been something about the way I said it that made the bigger leader (who I will designate as 'Big Ugly' from here on in) take pause and begin to think. "And how— pray tell," he asked with superiority in his voice as his cronies snickered in support, "could a Hog Farmer ever best one of us?"

"Well, let's look at the situation," I began to the steady creaking from the leather of my saddle as I brought my horse about in order to face them once again. "Your clothes are newer and better than what they have—why one can even tell what the original colors of yours are compared to the washed-out look of theirs. As such, you boys look much nicer than they do, so one could say you must be *prettier* than they are."

That brought a nasty look from Big Ugly.

Too bad!

"And just who would be saying that?" he demanded.

"That would be...me," I answered while preparing to sidestep my horse so as to back them into the corner once again. "Got a problem with that?" I questioned in such a way to let them know how an answer to my query would not be beneficial. Showing some restraint for the first time, the city lads remained silent; this allowed me to take the argument back to them.

"You say that the dirt on these boy's faces is an embarrassment to you and your city?" I asked amazed. "If the manner of dress of these two young lads is so important to you—as you five have graciously made yourselves official spokesmen for the rest of the inhabitants who reside here, then it is apparent that impeccable appearances are highly important to you," I observed logically. "I must say you place such an inordinate amount of importance on looks—so much so one would almost believe that you mimic the ways of pretty little girls more so than young men," I told him while trying to keep from laughing. "But if this is how the boys are in this city, then I guess you can be referred to in that manner if it is that important to you."

I could hear a short laugh coming from the direction of where Bryce was positioned, but I was not going to take my sights off these boys, so I would just have to assume it was him.

Big Ugly, along with all the smaller Uglies did not like what I had said one bit!

"Are you calling me a girl?" he wanted to know with menace dripping from his voice.

"Well, once again let's look at the situation," I answered him casually. "If you take a look at your hands, they are nice and soft from lack of hard work. These two boys have rough hands with calluses upon calluses from all of the work they must perform every day."

I tried my best to keep from smiling during my next comments, but my lack of success probably made Big Ugly even madder. "Even the girls of our town have rough hands from completing their daily chores," I explained. "The only ones that have such nice soft hands as yours are—the babies of the town."

This was getting to be too much for Big Ugly. I honestly believe that if I were not armed and on a horse that he would be going after *me* right then. Good; he was almost ready.

"So now we are girl babies?" he asked clenching his fists.

"No that's not what I said," I told him with maddening calm, "for if you *were* girl babies in reality, you would not accept a challenge to see if you Boys of the City were in truth more intelligent than these 'Hog Farmers' as you call them," I explained. "You *aren't* girl babies, are you?" I asked with contempt dripping from my voice.

Big Ugly just stood there among his stunned gang. I could tell that he knew I had backed them into a 'verbal' corner this time, with no way out.

"What manner of challenge do you propose?" he wanted to know. He was leery, yet his 'superiority' could not be questioned. After all, what could these uneducated field clods know that they did not?

"Tis a test; not of physical strength, but of mental ability," I informed them all while motioning for the Farmer boys to join us. "You may work together as teams, say you five against the two of them... unless you feel the need to go find more of you to make it fair," I observed.

Once again I got scowls for an answer, but no words.

"Fine," I announced, "for I do not have all day for you to try to find someone from among your circles who can match these boys when it comes to wits!"

Now call it a hunch, but I do believe these young city lads were not taking very much of a shine to me. I am certain I shall be able to get over my disappointment with time, I expect.

"So here is your challenge," I explained. "I will describe a situation, and you will have five minutes to come up with an answer.... best answer wins. Are you up for it?" I asked with eyebrows raised.

"Who gets to judge the quality of the answers?" he wondered, which I thought was a rather good question.

"That would be me," I answered him readily. "I am no 'Hog Farmer' as you have named these boys nor a man of this city, but rather a messenger for The Duke of Arlington Green. As such, I will be in earnest and fairly judge your efforts."

Turning about on my mount, I pointed to Sir Preston keeping his horse quiet directly behind me. "The man you see here is a Knight of the Realm, whom as you know has taken a vow to protect the sanctity of truth. His will be the final decision if I have ruled fairly or not."

"Shall we begin?" I asked while handing Miles a piece of cloth from my saddlebag to use for stemming the continuing flow of blood from his nose.

Big Ugly looked at his mates; one by one, each nodded their heads.

The challenge had been accepted.

"Here is the situation then," I told the expectant group of boys. "Each group of you has 10 silver coins to spend. The question to be answered is—how would you spend it so as to get the best return?"

Big Ugly looked at me with an expression of true surprise. "That's all there is to it?" he asked in laughter.

"The five minutes have begun," I announced curtly.

Both groups huddled together to plan their strategies. The City Boys argued back and forth, while the Farmers talked amongst each other while writing things down in the dirt so as to be remembered. They were still figuring things out when the city lads stood quietly in a circle looking confident and smug.

"What'cha doing?" Big Ugly asked the Farmers; "drawing stick animals?"

"No," answered Miles, "we are drawing a picture of your brain. The only problem is that we do not have a stick small enough to draw it to the proper size!"

Ooh...I liked *that* one.

Estimating the five minutes, I announced that time was up.

As they had more people, the city boys went first.

"We would take the 10 silver coins and go down to 'The Knights Inn' which is a very well-known tavern," Big Ugly said in confidence as spokesman for his group. "There we would spend the 10 silver coins on an excellent lunch with drink included," he said with pride. "As the tavern is almost always full, for us to be seen there would be an item for folks to talk about and remember for days to come."

"Very interesting," I commented once he had concluded his argument. "You would use the money for an immediate gain—which is a full belly… as well as a future gain—which would be bragging rights. Am I correct in my assessment?" I asked.

"That's it!" Big Ugly exclaimed to the nodding heads of his friends.

"*Very* interesting," I repeated. "And now to you Farmer boys; what would you do with *your* 10 silver coins?"

The younger brother Terrance spoke for the pair.

"We would take the ten silver coins and go down to the flour mill, where we would spend two of the silver coins on 10 pounds of flour," he explained. "From there, we would move to the mercantile shop and purchase 2 pounds of tea, a pound of sugar, and a bolt of cloth for 3 of the silver coins plus five pounds of the flour," he said while touching one different finger of his left hand with one from his right as he mentioned each item as if he were counting. "Our next stop would be the local chicken farm where we would purchase one rooster and two hens for the remaining 5 silver coins."

Miles took it from there.

"We would take all of our items home, where we would use about one pound of the flour, eggs from the hens, and some of the sugar to have our Mum bake us five cakes, which we would cut in half and sell for one silver coin per half. As Mum's cakes are well known" (*my* stomach can attest to that) "we should have no problem selling the lot," he reasoned. "Therefore, we would have the original ten silver coins back, four pounds of flour to make bread for our family for several weeks, 2 pounds of tea for our Mum and Dad, sugar for sweets for us all to enjoy, as well as the bolt of cloth for Mum to make herself and our little sister new dresses. Plus," he added proudly, "we would have the eggs from the chickens daily, and with the rooster there, eventually increase the flock. If we continued to repeat the process with our new ten silver coins in our pockets, we could utilize any materials which we already had to make additional cakes," he continued looking up at me as he explained his reasoning, "allowing us to eventually be able to save for a milk cow for the family."

Having completed his response, Miles looked over at the City Boys with his *own* self-superiority. Both of The Farmers looked pleased with their effort while the City Boys were stunned!

I took a short time as if considering the winner.

"Those were both some very interesting answers," I admitted; "congratulations to both groups. The Gentlemen from the city spent most of their effort on immediate gratification, for they do not have to worry about whether they will have enough food to eat tomorrow; they know *they* will not go hungry. The Boys from the country do not have such luxury," I said with a shaking of my head. "They must strategize on how to assure their family stability at the same time reacquiring their original investment and adding resources for the future. By re-investing their money and effort, they plan and *make* their own future, instead of waiting for it to hopefully occur."

"The winner—as I am sure all must agree," I announced to no-one's surprise, "is The Farmers."

There was no argument from the City Boys; they knew they had been beaten.

"So what do they win?" Big Ugly wanted to know. "Do they get to kick each of us in the tail while they are protected by their friends on horse?"

"And what manner of a victory would this be?" I asked. "All that would be achieved by that action is they would end up with hurt feet, and you City Boys would all get headaches!"

The Farmer boys chuckled at that one; I don't think the City Boys understood it.

"No; what they win is knowledge that while there may be people in this world who *have* more than they do, they are just as good as *anybody*! They have no need to hang their heads in shame, now or ever," I concluded.

"Come on boys," I urged the Farmers; "let's go home."

Both Bryce and I each carried one of the boys upon our horses to the stable where the carriage awaited us. For some odd reason, a small detachment of Royal Guards was loitering about outside of the stable. I thought no more of it, as we accepted the coach and headed for home.

Bryce drove the carriage, his horse tied to the rear of the coach. Sir Preston went on ahead, and I followed on my mount behind.

Inside the carriage were two young boys who never in their *wildest* dreams had even *imagined* they would get to ride inside of a coach as opulent as this! This had been a day that they would never forget!

As we approached the village, I rode ahead to speak to Sir Preston, then caught a word with Bryce. We took the long road and entered the town from the east. This way, everyone in the village could see the Farmer boys having a ride in The Duke's carriage. Their smiles as we dropped them off at their home were as warm as sunlight in summer!

We found The Duke anxiously awaiting us in the courtyard as we entered The Manor. "Why did you come in from the east?" he wondered, as we dismounted and re-arranged those parts of us that need to be re-arranged after the long ride home. "Were there any problems?" he asked with concern.

"No Sir," I answered him. When I explained the situation in the city; the more I spoke the angrier he became, for The Duke is proud of his village and especially the people who reside in it. When I told him of the outcome and the thrill for the boys to be seen in the coach, he agreed it was a fine idea, as I knew he would.

"Besides, Sir," I added with a broad smile. "What better way to reward the only two children in our entire school who received marks of 'excellent' for the essays which they wrote last week titled: *What Would I Do If I Were To Be Given Ten Silver Coins?*"

Made in the USA
Columbia, SC
03 September 2020